MW01485461

5

THE ARIMATHEAN

To Shannon —
Hope you enjoy
the trip . . .
Best —

A NOVEL

BY

SEAN LEARY

THE ARIMATHEAN is copyright 2012 Sean Leary. All material in this book is copyright 2012 Sean Leary. All rights reserved, including the right of reproduction in whole or in part in any form including book, audio, video, computer disc, CD-ROM, multimedia, blog, Internet, and all other forms, whether or not yet known or developed.

Material within may not be reprinted or broadcast without the express permission of the author, unless in a promotional capacity. If used in a promotional capacity, all work within must be credited to the author and it must be noted that the work appeared in **THE ARIMATHEAN** by Sean Leary. This book is published in the United States by Dreams Reach Productions and distributed worldwide by Ingram / LPI. The work is fictional. Any use of real names or details is speculative and in service of the fictional story and is not meant to be representative of factual events, nor should it be taken as such.

Very special thanks, as always, to my son, Jackson. Everything I do, I dedicate to you, my best friend and beautiful boy. I love you.

Very special thanks as well to Matthew and Pam Clemens, for your incredible support, advice and friendship. I'll never forget it.

Thanks as well to Connie Corcoran Wilson, Linda Cook, Sean Patrick, Jason Platt, Lindsey Joens, Bill and Gail Leary, Mary and David Stacel, Dan O'Shea and Johanna Harris, Trish Barker and all of my friends, fans and readers everywhere, particularly my readers and friends on Facebook.

ISBN # (eBook) 0-9772819-7-3

ISBN # (Print book) 0-9772819-8-1

Library of Congress Catalog Card Number: Applied for

First edition eBook: 10/13/2012

First edition print: 11/11/2012

Cover design by Jason Platt. Interior design by Sean Leary.

Website: www.seanleary.com. Email: seanleary@seanleary.com.

AS ALWAYS,

FOR JACKSON

WHAT CRITICS ARE SAYING ABOUT 'THE ARIMATHEAN'...

"This book rocks. That pretty much says it all. It just rocks. It really is a non-stop, action-packed popcorn book where the fun never ends. I enjoyed reading it immensely. I'm really looking forward to the sequels."

> --- *Matthew Clemens*
> *Best-selling author, "No One Will Hear You."*

"A real surprise, in a great way... a non-stop thrill ride of action! Full of huge thrills and stunning twists, smart writing and surprising heart. A book that will please action fans and fans of Christian fantasy alike, while pandering to neither. And in the end, a book of endless entertainment that makes you think, about life, about faith and about what drives us... a must-read."

> --- *Alison Baker*
> *Yahoo! News Chicago*

"Wow! Sean Leary is the new Stephen King."
> --- *Geeta Razack*
> *The Geeta Razack Blog*

"At first, when Sean Leary described his new novel 'The Arimathean,' I thought he had lost it. Ninjas and the Nativity – seriously? But he tells it here with seriousness and, above all, respect, with dialogue that fleshes out his characters and solid action that keeps the reader turning the pages. And don't skip to the last pages or you'll cheat yourself out of a finale that's truly grand."

--- Linda Cook
Award-winning critic / Iowa Press Women

"It takes a lively and inventive writer to cast the three wise men as ninja wizards. It takes a great writer to enrich and deepen such a high concept notion and create an exciting and compelling story as Sean Leary has done with 'The Arimathean.'"

--- Sean Patrick
Morning show host, WOC-AM

"Imaginative and moving at the same time."
--- Father John Comerford
Joliet Catholic Academy

"Lovely imagery… very nice descriptive turns of phrase."

--- Connie Corcoran Wilson
Best-selling author, "Hellfire and Damnnation"

"A bloody, gory, fight-filled adventure story… but here's the thing: this book is UPLIFTING. Gross at times, yes, intense throughout, definitely. But it also has that feel good quality a good adventure story must have. Whether you take that as a "Glory of God" message or just a "it feels awesome to kick evil's ass" message is up to you. The book puts no pressure on you to choose. Just enjoy the ride whatever way you want."

--- William Pepper
The William Pepper Blog

"An incredibly cool concept – ninja wizards for the win! – and an even more awesome book. It's not just an amazing idea that Sean Leary's got here, it's a rockin' adventure story with a ton of action, but a surprising amount of heart. It'll thrill you with its imagination and cliffhangers, throw you a ton of curves and leave you wondering what's going to happen next and then out of the blue make you really think about these people and feel for what they're going through. A masterfully written book."

--- Alternate Waves Comix Zine

FORWARD

I envy you, dear reader. You are about to embark on a wonderful journey, *The Arimathean*. I've read this book several times now, on its ten year journey from the mind of Sean Leary to the page.

It's a magnificent adventure that I would love to talk about more, but it will just slow you down (as well as not doing the story justice) on the amazing ride on which you are about to embark.

So, buckle in, hold on, and have a wonderful time. I hope you don't have anything planned for the rest of the night, you're going to be busy.

Enjoy,

Matthew Clemens
September 17, 2012

ONE

Awash in shadow jagged by light, surrounded by the soulless remains of men drowning the cries of their sins, he sat apart, alone, untouched by eyes and words. None dared to cusp his territory, as the tales that preceded him were enough to razor the spines of even these men whose hands had snapped bone and bathed in blood.

The dying day's choking sun coughed a dull, sanguine luminosity into the bar but it failed to venture anything but a sad, grasping hand towards the man slunk into the corner, whose presence was gouged into the room like a vicious scar.

His hair was dark and wild, askew and turbulent and torn as the thoughts rampaging beneath the weathered cage of his lined forehead. His face was drawn hard and forbidding, coiled in barely suppressed rage.

His body was thick and armored in muscle, undiminished despite his persistent attempts at ruin and drunken decay. Loose, earth-colored garments wrapped around him, caught by a thick brown belt of great weight, strapped with small satchels rumored to be containing a myriad of treasures, and sheathes harnessing deadly hunks of steel dangling ominously, blood-stained teeth waiting to sate themselves on the flesh of the unwise.

On those who would dare to challenge him.

Like a fang piercing the pale, a shadow penetrated the doorway of the dismal edifice.

A hulking figure eclipsed the fading light from outside, and into the hive of decay entered a monster of a man, encased in furs and metals, with a body full as a rhino and a cruel slit of a smile ripped across a face captured in jet-black barbed wire hair.

The men in the bar kept their heads to their drinks, their eyes darting like ferrets, through sideways glances, as they watched the grinning giant lumber in, making his way to the lonely table at the back. The goliath punished the ground with each step, through the gasp of the bartender and across the dirt and dust, over the grotesque pockmarks of crimson stains stubbornly refusing to fade from the floor, leading to the edge of the silent man's table. The dried, faded pools grew larger as the pariah's sanctuary loomed, the final destitute tombstones of men, arrogant, greedy and stupid, who had dared to challenge or threaten him, only to be thrown to the wild dogs and forgotten to the world.

The giant reached a pair of hulking arms behind his back and withdrew an axe the size of a lion.

He spit onto the fore of the table, a thick mass, black and bloody.

The man seated before the mountainous warrior looked up from his drink. His wizened eyes were flecked in gold, framed in sienna, the color of the line of horizon at dusk, where earth and heavens meet, cutting and alive, ethereal and aware.

"You are Arimathean?" the hulking beast growled.

The sitting man remained silent, lifting his glass and taking a swig, pursing his lips and grimacing as he set it down.

"You are Arimathean? You spawn of a diseased whore?"

The Arimathean's face stalked upward slowly, and for a moment, it met the larger man's, and, however slightly, the giant retreated.

"You know why I have come," the man with the axe growled. "Give them to me and I may let the wildlings drag your dead flesh until it is only half-eaten before buried."

The Arimathean's gaze pierced the goliath's stark, malevolent orbs.

The mammoth halted, then trembled, before regaining himself and clasping the handle of his axe tightly.

"Your powers hold no sway over me," the man said, in a deep, booming voice. "I have been trained in the clouded temples and carry some of the same charms."

He choked the leather of his axe and lifted it slowly.

"But not all," he spat. "Yet."

The seedy crowd dove for whatever cover could be found as with a mighty swing the cruel metal was hefted upwards and thundered down, exploding the table into a riot of shards.

But even more quickly, the Arimathean bolted from behind it, a split-second before his destruction.

A blur of steel sliced through the air!

Blood splattered and sailed about the room!

And then, with a sick thud, the armless, headless body of the mountain of man, his limbs scattered, his axe clattered impotently to the ground, slunk onto the dirty floor, melting into a slick pool of red.

The Arimathean did not bother to look down, kicking the dismal meat bag aside and reaching into a pouch on his belt.

He flipped a heavy, glittering coin to the bartender.

"I need another drink."

He looked down at the lifeless, gory lump of flesh, the once fiery, arrogant volcano of torso, and watched as a throng of rats the size of bread loaves scrambled to it.

"I would pay you for the mess," the Arimathean scowled, "but apparently that will not be necessary."

He grabbed his new bottle, took a long drink, looked around at the men, whose eyes feared his, and then he sheathed his sword and walked to another corner of the ramshackle bar, to another table, returning once more to the barbed womb of his Cimmerian solitude.

TWO

Six foreboding figures slathered in blood shambled towards the ivory palace, leaving gruesome red trails in their wake, their gory paths like a fresh wound carved by the teeth of a hungry beast.

They were tremendous and terrible, clad in stygian crimson and pitch black, torn garments that drooped heavy with gore over their hulking figures. Spikes split from their flesh and through their robes at awful angles and a field of ragged horns sat upon each of their shoulders jutting upward as wicked thrones for their grotesque reptilian faces. They bore slanted noses, snake slit eyes and their mouths were round and large, red lips broken and dry about rings of small teeth, like a lamprey's, surrounding a protrusion of mangled fangs jutting from the middle. Slick, black-skinned hoods dropped around the backs of their hairless heads like the crowns of cobras.

They were the D'hrhrough'Machkai in the ancient texts. In the human worlds, they were known as The Six.

Centuries-old mutations of subhuman half-demons, their hulking, decrepit forms grew more horrible, their visages more terrible to the eyes of man, as the hollow shells of their souls had become more tarred and molded with abominations performed.

They were mercenaries of the most diabolical order, enlisted by the shadow worlds of men for grotesqueries of occult nature. The means of compensation for their deeds were ritual perversions which fed the oily maws of the soul-possessing beasts slithering within them and sustained their power and presence in the human dimensions.

A trumpet announced their arrival and the gilded doors swung forward into an immense atrium buzzing with scurrying slaves and the clanking armor of soldiers at their posts.

A huge burgundy curtain parted behind a shimmering golden throne teeming with jewels as the reptilian ivory sliver of Ozmondias the seer emerged, the ice blue of his eyes and pallid glow of his face piercing through his billowy robes.

Moments later, with the lilting echoes of an orgy clinging, like red painted nails in his skin, behind him, King Herod strode from the curtains onto the throne arena. His tightly curled, burned-parchment hair and beard were heavy with sweat, his dark purple robes weighted with musky perfume on his sunburned, leather-skinned, hirsute bulk.

Whispers passed between the seer and his king as the latter settled onto his throne, inspecting a small, glass vial containing a scroll that was held before him by the seer. His face bloomed with an oily smile as he handed it back to Ozmondias, who secreted it into his cloak.

Herod smirked and turned to The Six, with a gleeful sigh.

``My friends,'' Herod purred to the man-beasts before him, ``I hear you bring good news.''

``Yes,'' the middle soldier smirked, holding aloft a dark velvet bag, a slow drip leaking from its bottom.

With a sideways glance from Herod, ten centurions, armor glistening, faces stony, strange medallions of silver and ruby gems about their necks, advanced from opposite ends of the palace, converging on The Six. One grabbed the bag, bringing it to Herod, the other nine stood, swords at the ready, three paces in front of the bloodied warriors.

Herod took a deep breath and trembled as he opened the bag slowly, inhaling its diabolical stench. He gazed upon its contents and a smile crept across his face. Reaching around within the bag, he ran his hands deliberately over its contents, his eyes aflame as they devoured all within. He glided his hand out, lifted it to his mouth and tongued the blood from it.

Still smirking, licking his ruby-slickened hand, he closed the bag and handed it to Ozmondias.

The vizier's long, spindly fingers closed like a viper around the satchel's throat, the tips of his other hand skittering along its edges, pale digits gingerly flicking along the damp passages. Then he opened it as well, his eyes aglow, his lips pursed and then curled into a smile.

``V'kk'nithr will be very pleased,'' Herod hissed, smiling. ``Very appreciative.''

``Yes,'' Ozmondias said, closing the sack slowly, leaning towards Herod, whispering in his ear, and then handing the damp pouch to an advancing centurion, who laid it upon a golden platter and disappeared behind the wine-colored curtain.

``You are satisfied?'' one of The Six growled.

Herod's eye met a line of servants to the left, sending them scampering. Seconds later they returned, followed by a dozen young concubines, their lithe bodies covered only in flamboyant painted marks and vibrant feathers of exotic birds, each bearing a shimmering box crusted in emeralds and rubies, each containing a squirming form in a tepid pool of blood.

The leader of The Six smiled, his pale fangs tongued clean and stark against his sallow reptilian face, dirtied and darkened by the ashes of bodies burned before it.

``And what is this unexpected surprise, beyond even our generous agreement?''

Herod's eyes slanted towards Ozmondias.

The vizier licked his lips and his eyes bored into The Six before him.

``We have…another job for you.''

THREE

Framing the night sky within two coarse, tanned, open hands, the man scanned the firmament slowly, stopping on an unusually bright star. One which, strangely, seemed even more vibrant than it had the night before.

He breathed deeply, ran his hands across the scruff of his beard and through his long, brown hair.

Taking one last glance at the brilliant ivory orb piercing through the darkness, he turned back to his home, to the kitchen, collected a hearty pot still warm. Placing it upon a wooden plate, he grabbed a cup of cool water and set it beside the earthenware and walked gingerly into the bedroom.

The woman smiled broadly as he entered the room.

"The storm seems to have passed," he said. "Only the distant thunder lingers."

"Good,'' she grinned. "Much better for the trip."

"Yes," he said, setting the dish down. ``Here, let me help you.''

He gently wrapped her in his arms, taking care of her bulging belly, and lifted her gingerly upward, allowing her to prop herself up against the meager cushions behind her. He ran a hand through her long, brown hair and gazed into her exotic emerald eyes before kissing her softly and smiling.

``Thank you,'' she said, kissing his cheek.

He kneeled beside her on the bare floor and brought the tray close.

``Are you sure you do not want anything?'' she began.

``No, no, no…'' he said. ``All for you. I want you to be as comfortable as possible.''

He placed the dish and cup on a slight table, sliding both easily within her reach. She took a deep drink of the water.

In a few liquid motions, with the ease of a man who'd done it many times before, he slid in front of her and began to slowly massage her feet. Her relieved sigh and the slump of her shoulders were all the reward he needed.

She blew a delicate wisp of steam off the bowl, took in its aroma, smiled softly and sipped.

``Mmm. This is delicious. What is in it?''

``Ancient secret,'' he smiled.

``From an ancient man,'' she giggled.

``Not that ancient,'' he laughed. ``Just a bit more so than you. But there is something to be said for experience.''

``Even if you have not shared many of yours with me,''
she raised an eyebrow.

``In time,'' he said. ``In time.''

``You are such a man of mystery,'' she said. ``But I am
glad you are mine.''

``Me too,'' he smiled.

``Oooh,'' she started.

``Feel a kick?''

``Yes,'' she said. ``He must like this tender loving care
as well.''

The man reached up and caressed her ample form,
following the small bump traveling across her round tummy like
a tiny wave.

``I love you, son,'' the man said.

The woman put her hand over the man's.

``Ohh!'' she said. ``He kicked when you said that. He
liked it. He always likes it when you say that.''

``I love you, son,'' the man repeated, following the little
foot shape lolling across her belly.

She motioned for her husband to move up next to her.
He cuddled up alongside, putting his arm around her as she lay
on her back, her head nuzzled to his chest, his hands stroking her
hair gently, her hand across his muscular arm wrapped around
her, protecting her.

"Promise me you will try to get some sleep," she said, softly. "I feel badly for waking you."

"I was already awake," he said, smiling.

"Watching over us?" she said. "Protecting us from the storm?"

"Always," he said, kissing her head.

``I love you.''

``I love you too.''

He held her close, and she gently fell asleep.

But he remained awake, watchful.

When he was satisfied she would not be disturbed, he slowly slipped away, laying her head down softly on her pillow and covering her with a thick blanket.

He strode surely, purposely, into the other room and just outside where a small, undistinguished mound lay apart from the house. He lifted it up to reveal a layer of camouflage, then another, and then finally an entrance to a space underground.

He looked around, then again, to see if he was being observed, but found nothing but stillness and the sounds of the night.

Quickly, he slipped into the hidden room.

He was gone only a few seconds, emerging with a dusty leather bag over one shoulder and a large white owl perched on his arm.

He stroked its feathers, spoke kindly into its ear, checked the cargo around its leg, released its restraint and patted it one last time before commanding it into the air.

``Away, Seraphim, away!''

With a mighty whip of its wings, the bird launched into the sky, lit by the eerie silver of the moon and the star that seemed to grow larger each time the man looked up at it.

The bird arced into the night and disappeared, as the man watched. And as the owl became a smoky sliver, the man scuttled to replace the hidden room's entrance, disguise it and quietly returned to the house.

He checked on his wife, looked back up through the window, at the night sky, once more measuring the unnatural orb's peregrination with a stretch of his fingers before him.

He lay down with his wife, holding her once more gently in his arms, caressing her full belly, and smiling as the child shifted.

``I love you, son,'' he smiled. ``I love you...''

The last word from his lips, before he slipped into sleep, was the name he and his wife had been given, just a few nights before, in dream.

"I love you..."

The name of their soon-to-be-born child.

``...Jesus.''

FOUR

The monolithic silver moon loomed a brilliant sentinel in the velvet void, leading a voluptuous chain of illuminants over the firmament, each growing in radiance in their ragged symphony from the earth to the swollen heart of the heavens.

The lightest, burned red, seemed to hover just above the blackened ground, pointing to a heavenly body just brighter above it, which gently sloped to a huge glowing orb which aligned, iridescent and bold, immediately below the moon, bulging and blinding, embracing the night with such radiance it rivaled the cusp of daylight.

The otherworldly chain, like fire off the eyes of lions in wait, glimmered over the land of the Watchers, the ones men called the Elohim.

Over The Glowing City.

S'iam B'ala.

Lit by the heavens, the skeletons of 10,000 men stabbed and jutted from the mountains surrounding S'iam B'ala. Its fortress was impregnable, in part because it remained directly unseen to the human eye (only visible through arcane tricks of perception known by an esoteric few), in part because its walls were steep, sharp and guarded by a field of marksmen who would scarcely allow it to be approached, let alone attacked.

Most left it to legend. Some tried in vain to conquer it or gain its mythical riches and power. Few had made significant inroads to find it, let alone mount an attack or gain entrance.

The interior of S'iam B'ala existed on a psychic and metaphysical dimension just above that of humans, and therefore few mortals could even muster the ability to enter it should it be found.

A series of intricate signs and gestures were required to communicate with those inside, to be awarded entry. And even then, one had to be pure of heart and mind to enter the center of its vibratory plane. The greater that gulf, the greater one's impurities, the more difficult it would be to remain within. Those impurities would keep one chained to the earthly plane and the dissonance between the two worlds occupied at once would subject the person to a growing, sharpening shriek sharding through their brain that would only grow in intensity until driving the human mind to madness.

One of the few to successfully accomplish the journey, make it into the Glowing City and remain was a holy warrior, whose amethyst eyes were devoid of human sight, but who, from birth, had been gifted with a vision beyond the crude dirt realm before her. Born of a sacred marriage, she became orphaned when her mother died at birth and her father shortly after. She had been raised in a clandestine monastery, trained in the ways of the N'nja, and had, since early childhood, felt a calling, to make the pilgrimage to the legendary city.

Upon the day of her thirty-third birthday, she began the journey to its mystical spires, guided by an occult sense beyond the ken of most mortals. She made the trek through the mountains and, eventually, the gates, where she excelled at all the tests placed before her and remained within the holy walls, until her death at the age of three hundred and thirty-three.

During her mortal journey, and legend has it, beyond, the ivory-and-silver clad mystic acted as a conduit between the two worlds, helping to forge communication between the Eternal Watchers within and an occult, chosen group of humans without, mortals who had been trusted disciples of the Watchers.

They were the ones who walked between worlds.

Who traveled among shadows bearing clandestine currencies.

Who stood above and beyond the realms of men.

The ones called Magi.

These men were considered great kings, visionaries and warriors among their people. They were incredible and cunning, both possessed of the deadly martial and mystic arts of the N'nja and the transcendent crafts of wizardry. They were human, and as such tethered to the earth and its brutal ways, but were footsteps from the gateways to the heavens and other worlds, able to traverse the gaps, albeit for the shortest of times, before being pulled back into their fleshen cages. As such, even after they had returned to earth, their lives moved at the loping pace experienced within the holy walls, and while those around them expired within a brutally short range of decades, they would often watch centuries pass.

Even so, they were human, and as such, the Magi could never fully know the glories of S'iam B'ala. Therefore the blessing of time in its glowing walls was intensely directed while their earthly selves allowed their presence in its hallowed halls.

Under the halo of moonlight on a night late in the ancient times, within the fortress, the sounds of swords slashed against each other and echoed against the imposing, storied stone. The men who had ascended to the highest levels of this secret society of wizardry and war engaged in the beautiful bounty of the art of conflict, training in its deadly trade.

They were wrapped tightly in the black robes of the sacred N'nja, the holy unspoken underground, of those who walked between the worlds, who dealt death to the flesh and souls of men, who were trained in the ancient arts, the ones called Magi.

They were three.

Gaspar.

Melchior.

Balthazar.

Thick as an ox, with rippled muscle bulging through his robes, Gaspar was possessed of an intimidating pillar of power upon which his gigantic, chiseled head rested. He was a massive trunk of a man, of foreboding presence and deadly girth, with olive skin smooth about a face like granite. His countenance was a severe, brutal beast made bearable only by soft, open eyes wide and expansive as the sky. Like the other two, he was a deadly swordsman and possessed of the arcane crafts, but his greatest potency was his strength, of mind and body, of more than a hundred men.

With a taut, feline air, Melchior had bare wisps of facial hair the color of the rusted skies of autumn carved upon his chin, a shaved head and a round, weathered face the tone of whipped sand and eyes of eerie silver-blue. He was a master of the ancient arts, possessed of countless totems and tokens almost as old as the world itself, and brilliant at the magick of energy, able to heal and kill with the touch of a hand, and manipulate all matter within his auric range, even to the point of opening doors between worlds.

Likewise wiry and blade-like in profile, Balthazar was the tallest of the three, with skin dark and smooth as a panther, sharp facial hair, a halo of ebony locks and a sleek, regal gait. His smile was generous, wide and inviting and his eyes tremendous and violet, lying like jewels amidst a throne of haltingly high and pronounced cheekbones and an aquiline nose. A cunning swordsman and brilliant scholar of the ancient arts, he was the most powerful wizard to stride the old worlds and into the new, able to travel between dimensions and bearing a majestic light and purity protecting him from the evils and manipulations of the demons within those nether realms, more than any mortal man before him.

They had been four, but one had fallen, driven aside, away into the realms of the heathen, never to return.

In their own time, the three, too, had descended, albeit temporarily, into their respective kingdoms, to rule as just men. They were called kings, but felt themselves keepers, sentinels of a justice, a peace, far beyond themselves, which they sought to transpose to their earthly realms.

But after years apart, away from the affairs of the world below, aside from those of their respective kingdoms, they were called. Called again to intervene as one in the ways of humankind and its comingling with the world of spirits. They were drawn by the stars, once more into the Glowing City, to prepare among the holy warriors of their formative years and then to descend once more, down into the world, the realm of men, the dirt of the earth.

They prepared as they always had.

In the fires of battle.

Among their own.

The three held their ground in the midst of the emerald training temple, surrounded by an army clad in the hallowed ebon robes. The Magi stood backs to each other, a triumvirate facing their attackers, their training swords drawn, as they surveyed the advance of dozens of fangs carved of aged wood, dual swords and nunchaku, bared before them.

On the call of a trumpet the hordes leapt to battle, and the Magi, swords at the ready, hurtled into action, a hurricane about them, countering strikes and delivering others.

Swords whirled towards Melchior as he traversed the maze of blows in a startling ballet, leaping and tumbling through and about the errant swings of challengers while dealing destruction in his wake.

Gaspar held strong against all comers, a massive boulder of a man, who watched as others' blades smashed and splintered against the force of his own, held steely in his grasp. With barely a flicker of his strength utilized to block the onslaught, the swords hurtling towards him would warp and crush against his steady weapon, causing a deep laugh to bellow from within him as he countered the lesser attacks with herculean blows of his own which sent his opposition barreling from him.

Balthazar's long sword was merely part of his parry against his encroaching pack, as he soared through their ranks, cleverly and deftly deflecting their advances while he wove smirking and sly enchantments at his attackers which would cause them to stumble, fall or collapse in the grasp of a power far beyond them. With a gesture, Balthazar would whisk them aside, the wizard hovering around the room, gliding about his pursuers, never allowing them to gain a bead upon him.

Brutal blades whipped through the air in a cacophony of conflict that the Magi traversed with incredible grace and devastating beauty, sending masses of warriors to the ground unconscious or groaning in pain.

Until finally, above them, on a balcony of marble, a gong was smashed and its echo was heard through the temple, three times.

As the first dirges of the copper orb rattled and shook, Balthazar whirled with lightning speed, his swords knocking away all those around him, as he propelled into the air, stopping and hovering more than the height of two men above them all.

His eyes glowed bright and with a flash he raised both hands. Immediately, the swords of the N'njas fighting the Magi burst into flame and smoke and disintegrated to black ash before them, causing the men, weary and chagrined, to halt and toss their useless hilts to the ground.

Balthazar descended to the temple floor again slowly, a smile upon his face, and looked to his two companions.

"We are summoned."

The three left behind the weary and beaten warriors and strode out of the emerald arena, amidst the ivory statues, the tapestries, gold and violet draping down mountains of silver and stone, columns the size of twenty men. They bowed at the eternal flame of the sacred traveler between worlds, Kailani X'ett, whispered her humble prayer, then continued past the reliefs and sigils carved into the walls, almost as old as the world itself in this mystical realm, half of earth and half of heaven.

They strode to the orb, the moonstone room, a tremendous oval, impenetrable and all seeing. There the oracles were arrayed in pools of orange and blue, in fragrant petals and illuminating plasma globs lit and hovering above them as they lay back in the waters, warm as the womb, secure in tremendous circular beds of pure ivory.

The three met their mentor, the Watcher, whose name was unspeakable to human tongues.

He was two feet taller than them all -- even Balthazar. He was of perfect features and eyes brilliant amethyst with tremendous dark seas of pupil, slanted in stunning horizons across his face. He was possessed of cheekbones and skin smooth and fine and lips of slightest pink upon flesh of a deep and creamy tan, hair of gold haloing it, above a body of taut and lean muscle clad in robes of the purest white adorned with the holograms of silver and gold and Sanskrit and ancient codes hovering above and around him.

The three crossed the room to him and together they ascended a spiral staircase to an aviary on the roof, lit by an array of torches and attended to by several others in robes of the lightest blue.

The men looked to the heavens, then to the clerics manning the cages. With a nod from the Watcher, the cages were opened and armies of doves – black, red and white – flooded the sky.

Each bird was svelte, elegant and strikingly plumed with long, lush feathering. Each was emblazoned with a tiny, barely perceptible birthmark in the shape of a clandestine sigil scrawling along the cowl of plumage behind its right eye. And each had a small scroll bearing a coded message secured tightly around its left leg.

The men looked as the birds broke against the light of the mammoth moon and disappeared into the night. They watched and stared, at the heavens above, at the line of three stars, each more brilliant than the other, the celestial path marking the way to eternity.

Then, with the birds dissipated into the distance, the Magi turned to the Watcher, the man whose name could not be spoken in human tongue. They heard his words in their minds, calm and serene, as a parchment being slowly unfurled.

He regarded them with a knowing glance.

They returned with subtle bows in honor as they turned and left, descending the heights of the aviary.

"So it is time," Gaspar said. "To return."

"And none too soon," Melchior said. "The black hand could only be deceived for so long before it began to close around our quarry."

"We can only hope it continues to be so misled," Gaspar said.

"It will be," Balthazar said. "For now, but for little longer."

"So we leave?" Melchior began.

"Within the hour," Balthazar said. "Tonight."

FIVE

The boys' eyes furtively darted about the hearty,
raggedly stocked shop, lingering on the drooping, elderly keeper,
seemingly oblivious, his head over a scroll, his thick lips
bobbing slowly as his aged eyes digested it.

With a jerk and a shove, they were off, hands full of ripe,
juicy contraband, tearing towards the door.

They were seconds, seconds away.

Sweaty and smiling.

Giggling and gleeful in victory.

Or so it seemed.

With one fluid move, the shopkeeper raised his gaze,
and his arm, and sent a rock zipping towards a latch above the
exit, nailing it and sending a gate soaring down, over the door,
trapping the would-be thieves in their tracks, stunned and
breathing heavily, caked in nervous sweat.

Their shoulders slumped, they surrendered to the smirking man.

"You have something you would like to return to me?" the man reprimanded.

The boys' mitts opened to reveal several small breads and dried fruits.

"We are sorry, sir," one boy meekly offered.

The man looked over the would-be thieves, saw the gaunt sallowness of their cheeks, the hollowness of their forms.

"Are you hungry?"

The boys shrugged, ashamed to answer.

"Here," the man offered, returning the items to the surprised duo.

"Eat."

The boys looked at each other, then the man.

"Go ahead."

They looked at the food, hesitant.

"I will say it no more! Eat!" said the older man.

The boys dug in, ravenously.

"You are Philip and Andrew, are you not?" the older man said, crossing his arms over his chest. "Your father is a fisherman? Your mother was just blessed with a new boy?"

The two, dusty and ragged, looked at the man with slight surprise.

"Yes, that is us," Philip said.

"I am in need of two helpers, perhaps boys of quickness and cunning such as yourselves, in my shop," the man said. "I cannot afford to pay much, but your bellies will not go hungry in my employ. Nor will your family's. And you will no longer need to risk thievery."

The boys looked at each other.

"Thank you sir, we would most appreciate that," Andrew said.

The man nodded to them, then to the baskets arrayed before them.

"Fill your pockets, and your bellies, and I shall see you when the sun is up again," the man said, smiling.

The boys hesitated only briefly, before scurrying to jam as much as they could into their dusty, ratty cloaks.

"Thank you sir! Thank you very much!" Philip said.

"Yes, thank you! God bless you!" Andrew said.

The man lifted the gate and latched it again in place, above the door, leaving the portal open and nodding and grinning to the boys, who beamed in return and ran towards the exit and into the street.

"Tomorrow! As the sun rises!" the man called after them.

"Tomorrow!" Andrew called back.

"Thank you sir!" Philip said.

"Thank you!" Andrew echoed.

The boys disappeared down the street and the man shook his head and rolled his eyes, with an amused grin, returning to his shop and his scrolls.

A wind blew through from the back of the space, chilling him and lifting gooseflesh on his skin. Thinking he had left a window open, he strolled to the flank of the market.

At the front, his gate slammed shut.

"Boys? Is that you?"

The man looked around his shop, watched the floating dust particles suspended in the beams of sunlight hovering in.

"Are you playing tricks on an old man?"

He heard a deep, crackling voice.

"Nothing quite so kind and playful, Bartholomew."

He whirled to see the last lazy rays of daylight eclipsed by three massive figures before him, a pyre of horns and hoods conjoined, a darkling mask curtaining the sun's wheezing embers at their flanks.

His hand went to his sword but it was seized by a massive claw grasping him hard from behind.

His other hand streaked to his knife but it was locked in a steel grip from yet another demon behind him.

The Six slimily enveloped the shopkeeper, encircling him like a boa choking its prey.

"We know who you are, Bartholomew Levi, of the silent hand," one of the demons rasped, "and you know why we are here. Give us the information we seek and we may leave you merely maimed or deformed, but alive."

"What information?"

The lead demon expelled a heavy, pungent breath of rancid aroma.

"We have no time for façade, nor will you insult us by insinuating such," the demon hissed. "You have information we seek. You know the whereabouts of the ones we seek. We know you have it. And we know you will surrender it to us, or forfeit your life."

"I am certain you have me confused with another," he said.

"We are certain we do not."

The demons' claws closed harder around his arms, causing them to bend inwards sickeningly, giving way and cracking.

"I will never talk!" Bartholomew shouted. "I will die first!"

One of The Six clasped a scaly, razor-taloned hand around the man's neck, crushing forth only a pathetic gurgling from his lips.

"You are right on both counts," the demon hissed. "You will die and you will never speak again."

A second demon hovered his drooling mouth over the man's face, dripping viscous goo over it. His thick, leechlike lips bulged and protruded, and a set of smaller jaws on a stalk-like maw ribbed with tiny teeth extended down, down, towards the man's panic-frozen countenance.

The first beast, his claw still grasped around the man's neck, used his other hand to squeeze in the man's cheekbones, forcing the victim's mouth open wider, wider.

"There, there," the demon hissed.

"Thankfully, we do not need you to talk to gain the information we seek," the first demon purred, and began to cackle as the second demon's protruding, serpentine jaw appendage slithered into the human's mouth and down his throat. The hell spawn's mucus-laden tongue pushed and stabbed deeper, deeper, causing Bartholomew's eyes to roll back in his head as his body seized with the pain of the demon's proboscis burrowing, burrowing, burrowing, slimily up into his sinus cavity, and finally, poking, stabbing, into his brain, where it slithered around slowly and embraced the soft, vulnerable flesh like a lover.

"Yessss, yessss," the first demon hissed, as his probing brethren's eyes slowly spun back in his head, veins spider webbing the orbs in his eyeholes as he lapped up the information he required.

And when he was sated, his proboscis withdrew, and the first demon hissed, his grasp tightening slowly, slowly, crushing the old man's spine.

"Yessss, yesssssss," the demon whispered into the dying man's ear, as he felt Bartholomew's fragile human bones crack in his massive hand. "Yesssss."

SIX

It was the heart of the night when the Arimathean stumbled from the door and onto the filthy streets. The moon was a titanic, lucent eye, looming over a luminous pearl of a star and two others, less brilliant but still striking, dripping below.

As he walked through the decaying town, illumined by the heavens and the crumble of a strange, distant lightning, he noticed the remains of his evening collapsed and discarded in the alley, distracting him for a moment.

A breeze caught him.

His nostrils flared.

He quickly turned, sword drawn, as the night rang with the clash of steel against steel.

And then, with the sound of laughter.

"Balthazar," the Arimathean said, as he lowered his sword and sheathed it. "I knew it was you."

"Your abilities remain sharp," Balthazar said.

"No," the Arimathean said, "My nose just cringed at the overpowering stench of patchouli."

Balthazar smiled and the two men next to him laughed.

The three advanced, surrounding the Arimathean.

The Magi were no longer clad in the dark warriors' garb of the N'nja. They wore the murky, richly colored, liquid robes of noblemen, bound with gold ropes and fine leathers and adorned with shimmering, morphing stones of occult nature.

They smiled as they greeted the Arimathean, Balthazar placing a long-fingered, spidery hand upon his shoulder.

"It is good to see you again, my friend."

"I wish I could say the same," the Arimathean said. "What do you want?"

Gaspar laughed deeply.

"He knows us too well," he said.

"And we, him," Melchior smiled.

The Arimathean shot a slanted glance at him.

"You did," the Arimathean said. "Not anymore."

Balthazar grinned.

"Only God can claim such certainty in any matter, my friend."

"He could," the Arimathean said, spitting on the ground. "If He existed."

He looked the three over, and then gazed hard at Balthazar.

"We need your help, my friend," Balthazar said.

"What a surprise," the Arimathean grumbled, turning to walk away from them.

"But it is not only for our sake," Melchior said. "The world needs . . ."

The Arimathean boiled in anger.

"To hell with the world!"

"But . . ."

"I do not want to hear it, Balthazar! Not again. Not anymore. The world can die for all I care and all of humanity with it. It will not be mourned. Not by me, at least."

He stormed away.

"How can you turn your back?" Gaspar said. "How can you, once one of us, refuse the calling?"

"Because I did not refuse it before, when I should have," the Arimathean said, spinning back to them. "I helped you, I helped your God and He did nothing to help me. He did nothing but destroy the life I had. And unless you can give me that chance again, to make a different choice at that time, you have nothing to change my mind."

Balthazar traded glances with Gaspar and Melchior.

"Herodius," Melchior said.

The Arimathean stopped.

He looked down.

Grimaced.

Spit onto the ground.

Remained.

The three advanced to him, and Balthazar put his hand on the Arimathean's shoulder, smiling.

"Walk with us," Balthazar offered, as they proceeded into the night. "Again."

SEVEN

They had little to take, nothing to leave behind, not much to start. It was still night, a few hours before dawn, still cool, before the scalding sun would hound them, when Joseph fastened their packs to the horses and his back, made Mary as comfortable as possible and embarked upon their trek.

He began the journey slowly, allowing her to maintain a restful state, kissing her forehead and lips and bulging belly, looking ahead, holding her hand. She was a slight woman, with delicate features, shimmering dark auburn hair and wide, warm, pond green eyes, a kittenish demeanor of vulnerability and kindness. She was petite and ethereal, and it was something of an incongruity to see her, at first glance, with the weight of a child around her. Joseph was far taller and more substantial, tawny and taut with muscle, with sun-worn skin and heavy, thick, earthen colored hair. She rode upon the first horse, the more sturdy and steadfast of the two. Joseph rode the second, barely beyond a mule, beside her.

As they traveled, the morning sun was a soft caress across the pinks and purples and oranges drifting amidst the wide blue sky, a deceitful peace that was a duplicitous harbinger for the harsh heat that would beat down upon them just hours from now.

Mary tried to gain some rest, tried to remain calm, to enjoy the quiet gallop beneath the beatific dawn.

The census order that had led them to this trek had come down a few weeks before. The messages had begun three weeks before it. Messages, through dreams, but dreams unlike any other, clear and tangible, able to be felt with a disturbing resonance when daylight broke again.

As a result, her thoughts were troubled, her sleep restless. She was hopeful, happy, upon the news delivered to her. But once she considered the consequence, the resistance she and her firstborn were destined to face, she quaked and stirred sleepless with dread, fearing what was to come. Finally, upon contemplation, prayer and visitation of a comfort and force far beyond her, she surrendered to faith, to a knowing, a steadfast belief, that despite the obstacles ahead, all would be made right.

Still, she remained unable to rest with complete ease. She was human, after all, and could not bear to consider their baby, the wonderful life growing within her, to be threatened or harmed in any way. Faith would sustain her, yes, but even the faintest contemplation of the alternative would brush her with sadness and burden her sleep.

Perhaps it was illusion, perhaps some strange means to lull herself, but in the half-in, half-out mists of slumber, in the middle of the night, she would imagine Joseph leaving their bed, going to the windows and visiting birds.

Owls, if she woke by night.

Then, if she napped by day, doves.

Strange.

And ironic.

For it had been birds that had brought them together.

"I built this for you," Joseph had said to her, several months before, holding a fine, sturdy wooden aviary, with room for several birds and accoutrements for food and water.

She smiled. "Thank you."

They had spoken only briefly prior. He had moved to her town just a while before that. They had exchanged friendly greetings, polite acknowledgements while stealing glances from afar, keeping a tentative distance from one another, uncertain, nervous.

"I noticed you, and the children, tending the birds, the wounded and the sick," Joseph said. "I thought you could use it.

It may make it easier to keep them sheltered, from the predators that would prey upon them while unattended."

"It will be of great help," Mary said, looking it over. "It was kind of you to notice, and it looks very well crafted. Thank you."

Joseph nodded.

A few of the children of the village bombarded Mary with hugs and giggles, running about her as they played an impromptu and short game of hide and seek behind the billows of her dress, circling her with bounds and chortles as she and Joseph laughed at the younglings' imagination and zeal.

"You are very good with the children," Joseph said.

"I love children," Mary said. "They are innocent, blank slates. They reflect what they are shown. If you treat them with kindness, they will learn that, and spread it to their worlds. If only you allow them to feel that love, allow them to feel safe in sharing it."

"I admire your patience and caring," Joseph said. "I admit, I am a bit taken aback by it. I have traveled for quite a while and unfortunately my experience with mankind has not been quite as affirming as it has been the past few weeks here watching you."

"I appreciate your kind words," Mary said. "But I have to admit I am only doing what God would have me do."

"But it is what so few would do, regardless of God, or His purported place in their life," Joseph said.

"He has done so much for me," Mary said. "I see the birds, see how He cares for them, the slightest of His creatures, and have no fear that He would protect me the same way. He would put others into my life that would give me shelter or help, the same He has brought me into theirs."

Joseph smiled softly at her. She returned the warm look upon his face.

"Perhaps you are right," he said. "Perhaps He would. For you."

He reached down then, at that moment, and touched her hand, for the first time, and just for a moment. Her heart jumped. Like never before. But she said nothing to him, only fled from his glance, her head down, afraid to meet his eyes.

He nodded to her, she to him, and he walked away, turning back a few strides off, to capture her glance again, to bask in her, before he strode back to his work. He watched as the children once more buzzed about her, enveloping her in their infectious glee, and she smiled as she watched him work, hoping she would talk to him again, soon.

She remembered that day, remembered the place they had first spoken, that he had first touched her.

And she had looked back upon it, looked upon the town as they had left it, looked back upon their humble but sturdy home, and smiled.

It was an unassuming hovel, barely noticeable, certainly nothing one would marvel upon at first glance. But it was magnificent upon closer inspection. Stable. Secure. Comfortable. Like him.

He had built it by hand, with rough strength and supple, clever dexterity. Another of the many things she admired about him.

She would miss it. She would miss home. But the trip had to be taken and she felt safe with him by her side. No matter what, she knew he would protect her.

But from what he would have to protect her, she could hardly imagine, even among her deepest trepidation, or her darkest nightmares.

EIGHT

A staccato line of torches burned along the temple walls, staunching the flow of the saturnine dim outside and within and illuminating the fresh corpses of the men slumped to the floor below the grotesque, leering forms of The Six.

Three priests had been kept separate from those slain. Kept alive. Each stripped and strapped to different corners of the altar, so they could not see the others, but could each hear the cries of the other men as The Six tortured them, one at a time, until their pleadings were drowned in blood and they melted away, silent.

The third, and last, had proven remarkably resilient.

They were holy men, blessed and sanctified, and thereby immune to the more insidious means of interrogation available to The Six. An invasion of the body and mind, as the demons had performed on the handful of unfortunates leading to this point, would do little but offer physical abuse and death, as the priests' auric shields would deflect any attempts at psychic theft.

However, the priests, despite their discipline and piety, were human. And the demons knew, thereby they were ultimately fragile beings, able to be broken.

It was somewhere near the sixth hour of perversions and defilements, shortly after the bloody faces of his brethren were lifted and scratched and ripped along the walls to write vile demonic sigils that the final barrier snapped in the psyche of the third priest.

He was left alive long enough to sputter the few words needed, then slain with a razor-sharp claw across his neck.

Their information finally procured, their initial quest finally completed, The Six sent word to Herod, dispatching a cadre of ravens to deliver it. The demons camped in the temple, feasting upon the slain, awaiting word on their next mission.

Soon, the Six were joined by a massive army of centurions under their command, sent by Herod, and they set off into the last hours of darkness, to follow a new path, of fresh destruction and conquest.

"By the fall of three nights hence, all shall be ours," the leader of The Six purred to his brethren, "in chains, or in death."

NINE

On the horizon, the tent appeared slim and fragile, nothing but a weakly glowing lantern amidst the storm ripping the void of the night. However, within, it was starkly calm and warm, eerily so, kept still and serene through minor enchantments.

The four men sat around a meager fire which remained a low blaze, unhindered and unmoved by the rampage outside. They drank thick, spiced wine and the three mages spun stories as the Arimathean listened, stoic, silent, and gulping from a large bottle.

"You are very quiet, my friend," Balthazar said to the Arimathean.

"You hardly need my words to fill the air."

Gaspar laughed.

"What the hell do you want me to help you with?" the Arimathean said. "And how will it help me get to Herodius?"

"You will see soon enough."

"Not soon enough for me," the Arimathean said. "Tell me why you are here."

"We are here to protect one who cannot protect himself," Melchior said. "But one who must be protected."

"And how do I fit in? You hardly need me to safeguard you."

"We are strangers here," Gaspar said. "We cannot hide. And we cannot lurk in shadow in attempting. Not any longer."

"Why not? Somebody find you already?"

The three shot glances at each other, silent.

The Arimathean sighed.

"And you need me to do what, pose as a translator or guide or something?"

The three men exchanged glances again.

"In order to move freely about, especially during this time of census, we. . ." Melchior began.

"We need you," Balthazar said, "to pose as a nobleman. A local, returning to his place of birth, for the census. With us, properly cloaked and disguised of course, as your attendants and guards."

"The ruse would allow us to follow the same path as our quarry, and would explain any actions that may need to be taken," Melchior said, "as well as allow for any, persuasion that may be needed to take place."

The Arimathean steeled his gaze at them.

They looked at each other, and back at him. He smirked at their robes of fine silks, their bejeweled belts and exotic scabbards, and the sharpness of their features and facial hair.

"Yes, I can see where you may stand out here," he said. "But only just a bit."

He laughed.

The three looked at each other, then at the Arimathean, and joined him, slowly, in laughter. And as they guffawed, his own merriment faded and turned to a smoldering darkness that exploded in fury.

"Enough!"

He glared at Balthazar.

"This is not going to work," he said. "I care little about your stories or your jokes or your pitiful attempts to make me a human being again. I want Herodius. That is it. You tell me where he is and when he is returning from the East and by what path. I will find him and kill him."

"You will, will you?" Gaspar scoffed.

The Arimathean glared. "Try me."

"Even if you do manage to get through his armies and kill him, your actions will not bring you peace," Melchior said.

"I do not want peace," the Arimathean said. "I want revenge."

"And then what?" Gaspar said. "As Melchior noted, astutely, I might say, Herodius will not travel alone. You will have to fight an army to get to him, which will leave you spent before you even think of clashing swords with the one you seek, who is a formidable foe alone. And even if you make it through to him and somehow manage to defeat him, then what do you hope to find? A noble death? For a man so defiant of an afterlife, and so dirtied of actions in this realm, you seem oddly certain you will find what you want there."

The Arimathean gritted his teeth, his face a clenched fist.

He lunged at Gaspar, but the larger man caught his blow with a quick whip of his massive hand, and then clasped another around the neck of the smaller man. But he wasn't fast enough, and the Arimathean whirled his free hand to his belt, unsheathing his knife and bringing it to Gaspar's neck, pressed tight to his jugular.

The Arimathean froze, and shook, and his hands loosed and he dropped the knife, and fell to the ground, limp.

Behind him, Melchior waved his hand casually and the Arimathean convulsed back to life, coughed and shook himself up, sheathing his knife and turning to Melchior, who glided up, looming over him.

"This conflict helps no one," Melchior said.

"I will find Herodius myself," the Arimathean spat. "Good luck with your . . . mission."

He pushed out of the tent, into the storm, and almost instantly, it sealed back up, leaving the three in the disquieting calm.

"He will be back," Gaspar said, rubbing his neck.

"Maybe," Melchior added. "Maybe."

He looked at the third man. "Balthazar?"

"Destiny follows its own path," Balthazar said. "As do we."

"And what about the path of the one, of the ones, we are here to protect? How do we follow that without revealing our presence?"

Balthazar sighed and put a hand to his chin.

"I have a feeling," Balthazar said, "the answer will reveal itself sooner than we think."

"But in the meantime?" Gaspar said.

"They are safe," Balthazar said. "But we must find them, for that safety will soon come to an end."

TEN

The road was slow, even slower than expected, given Mary's condition. The heat exhausted her, caused them to stop and seek shelter, seek sustenance, as often as possible. It would cause their plans to alter dramatically, their ambitious schedule of arrivals to become more than slightly abridged.

But Joseph was always patient, always kind, never one to utter a cross word or usher her on, regardless of any imminence he may have felt within.

He had been remarkably understanding, faithful, in the midst of their personal storm. He had always shown a temperate disposition, which is one of the things which drew her to him. However, it was beyond so mundane a form of explanation as mere patience, or even devotion between a husband and wife. She realized that few men, perhaps none but him, would have displayed quite the temperament he had, considering the fantastic circumstances of their lives.

Yes, he had the dream, the same vision, as her. But so many men would have dismissed it. So many men would have left. So many men would not have believed. They would have folded under the constant looks, whispers, backdoor condemnations, and the unmistakable weight of the judgments of their neighbors.

But not him.

It was as if he knew. He had that calmness of being. He knew. The truth.

As did she.

And as with so many things, it only made them closer.

As with so many things.

She remembered the first time she saw him.

He had been in her town for a short time before they met. Word had spread of the handsome stranger, a young man, of only a few more than two decades passed, but one of a wisdom far beyond his years, and a bearing of striking resonance. Dark haired and dark eyed, with a rough beard and a tall, sinewy stature, riding in on the cusp of night, on, some said, a camel.

He cut an exotic figure, carved all the more impressive and mysterious by the incessant chatter of the women of the town, buzzing about, filling the air around Mary and her family and friends with their gossip and stories.

Some said he was a soldier from a foreign land.

Others a member of the silent hand on a sub rosa mission.

Still more merely placed him as a merchant, a carpenter, making his way into a new town looking for work.

However, those more pragmatic designations only seemed to emerge upon later days, as the man blended into town. And they bloomed almost as an envious reaction to the amazing tales initially posed but never corroborated. So she was never quite sure what to expect from this near-mythical figure who had been so dauntingly drawn before her.

When she finally saw him, it was a far different man than the rakish rogue of the women's dreamy passages.

She woke to find him, sweaty and dirt-caked, outside with her father, the two of them working intensely to repair a cart which vandals had destroyed. She and her mother brought the two of them cool water and light refreshments. And when her eyes met with the stranger she felt unlike she had ever before, as if the world had become abuzz, her chest tingling, her eyes shyly drawn to his, unable to look away once caught.

The man, Joseph, would remain in town, setting up shop as a carpenter, and living considerably less fantastically than the advance rumors would have had it. He was unassuming, quiet and polite, sturdy and kind, and unrelentingly proper and respectful.

Before long, their love was in bloom.

They shared rich conversations during his brief respites from work. He was guarded, tentative, measured in his tales of his own life. However, he was always an attentive listener, with a dry wit and a gentle nature, which complemented Mary's playful humor and open, loving way. They would often play with the neighborhood children, or he would watch as she read to the young pupils, or taught them the skills of the home, as he would offer lessons in the basics of his trade. At the end of the day, as the children faded to their respective homes, Joseph and Mary would watch the sunsets, marveling at the beauty and unique majesty of each day's denouement.

The years between them mattered little, and seemed of no consequence to either, given the easy, joyful connection, attraction and camaraderie between them. Ultimately, they shared the same want, of a quiet, humble life, ripe in the happiness of family and home.

Having been together a suitable time of courtship, Joseph humbly asked Mary's father for her hand in marriage.

Her father was apprehensive, her mother less so.

"Why do you doubt him?" her mother asked. "You, who have spent more time with him than most?"

"I do not doubt his sincerity, or his integrity, or character," her father said. "He is a fine man, a just man. But he is almost twice her summers, a man, a man of the world. And Mary, she, I love her, I love her with all my heart, but she is just beyond a child, a girl, an innocent clad in woman's clothes. And Joseph, while a good man, is a man. He knows the ways of the world, the ways of men."

"She is no longer a child, and has not been for quite a while," her mother said. "You are right, she is a pure heart. But a pure heart that knows what it wants, and perhaps knows best. You admit he is a man also of fine character. She has chosen well."

"I am, still uncertain," her father said. "Perhaps Mary is best with a boy, one of naïve and idealistic ways. One with whom she can run along parallel paths to adulthood."

"Or one with whom her innocence will be disregarded and misunderstood, taken for granted and broken, as his is as well?" her mother said.

"Perhaps," her father said, wearily. "Perhaps you are right."

"Which man holds his treasure closest to his heart?" her mother said. "The one who has been raised among rubies, or the one who has seen diamonds run through his fingers and finds himself holding one once more?"

Her father passed his hands across his beard, contemplating.

"You are right, my love, you are wise."

"Mary is an innocent," her mother said. "She knows little of the evil men can do. Who best to be with her, to protect her and help guide her, than a man of wisdom who has seen the world and knows its ways? Knows where and how to protect her and will do so with every essence of his being?"

Her father looked upon his eldest daughter, caring for her younger siblings tenderly.

"Look at her," her mother said. "She is of a giving, generous way, in large part because we have sheltered her and allowed her to be so. She has remained such a wondrous, loving heart. She has never known the attentions of another.

"Think about this man, his quiet, calm demeanor," her mother continued. "His travels, his scars, his tales. His thirst for peace which brought him to our town. He is a man who would be patient and kind with her, who would cherish her for who she is, recognize and appreciate it.

"Now think about Mary's other potential suitors," her mother said. "They may be of good homes, may have good hearts, but they are callow and green, innocent but unknowing. Would they make a better match for her? Would they give her the patience she needs?"

Mary's father acquiesced the next day.

They had planned to be married shortly after.

It was shortly before the marriage that the event occurred.

At first, Mary believed it nothing but a fantastic dream.

But then, she had another, more realistic, more specific in details, instructions.

And then, the symptoms began, the dreams, the visitations arrived on a more regular basis, and she knew it was nothing of her imagination.

She was with child.

When she first told her parents, and Joseph, they were conflicted, saddened and torn. Their faith told them to believe, but their humanity did not. Their experience with her was certainly none that would bespeak of any impurity or infidelity, but her kindness, her heart, was likewise one that would not cause to condemn any man which would take ill advantage upon her. So great was her capacity for love and forgiveness, they thought she may have been attempting to hide the imposition of a lower man, knowing full well that if his crime were exposed he would be run through and his burning body would be hanging from the lurching tree outside of town before the following nightfall.

Love led Joseph to remain, to trust, to have faith. To believe that this, too, was part of the destiny for which he had been drawn to this town, to these people, to her.

She had always insisted that it was best to have faith, regardless of how one's plans may go awry, or seem halted. To have faith in God and in your ability to find the right path and blaze upon it, for it would only be in retrospect that one would realize the true reason for those diversions which seemed like impediments at the time.

And so he resolved to remain by her side, but was still uncertain as to the nature of her condition, unsure of the phenomenon of which she insisted.

That night, Joseph, and Mary's parents, were each visited, as Mary had been, in dream, and when they woke the next day, they believed.

The marriage was performed immediately.

"Would any other man have stood so strong and steadfast by her?" her mother said to her father shortly after they were wed.

Her father shook his head. And smiled.

"We chose sagely and kindly," he said, holding his wife close. "Thank you, for your wisdom, and your stubborn nature."

Mary and Joseph thanked them for their blessing.

They kissed and embraced.

They were one.

And now they would be joined by one other.

One other, who was furtively kicking away, as they began on their trip, talked of its intricacies, its planning, its necessary requirements for their safety.

Preparations were already in motion, in anticipation of the birth. But the census order came as a bit of a shock, a suspicious one at that, and left too much to chance, too much to risk.

Any journey in these times, particularly one of length, one which needed to be traversed so slowly and carefully with a woman in Mary's condition, was fraught with potential danger.

All the more so this time, she felt.

And all the more for the hidden perils that could be lurking at any way along the path due to the specific and unusual nature of her condition.

There were signs, cues, secret gestures and glances that were made open to Joseph, that could help them along the way. But given the iron fist of control exerted by Herod and the Empire, the totality of their armies, the best Mary and Joseph could hope for was anonymity for as long as possible.

They would arrive at a modest home in a town they would reach by nightfall. Not the town Joseph had ambitiously planned to make, but a secure location. It would be marked by the sigil that had been placed on the overhang of the roof, gently hovering, and the couple would remain there until such time as it was safe to continue. And they would continue along those same clandestine paths, remain in shadow, as needed, to avoid the surveillance of the Empire.

If they could make it to birth it would be a miracle.

But that is precisely what they were hoping for.

ELEVEN

Above a heaving landscape the color of bile and blood, a wriggling morass of disgusting, ashy, bat-like creatures with veiny, translucent wings carved the air. Their thrusting pockets of flesh belched a sick, puking sound across the horizon as they shoved the beasts' horrible, distended gullets across a sky of ochre and gray, scratched by the moans of dead souls blistering in welling clouds of flame.

The sounds of whips and shrieks scarred the air along with a nauseating stench, as corpses, spent by demons of torture, fell fresh to the ground, to be kicked by excrement-caked hooves and devoured by creatures of nightmarish grotesquerie.

Cracking the clouds, came a blinding illuminant, violet and rose and gold, and a woman, clad in white and silver warrior's robes, breathtakingly brilliant, floating so slowly, descending almost imperceptibly, from the rift in the heavens.

As she wafted downward, her luminosity was an umbrella to the sky and ground and caused its bleakness to fade, as if covered by gauze, slowly, slowly, to white, and clear.

The agonized wails turned to sighs. The ground heaved open and the demons and harpies fled into the diseased womb of their demise.

As the woman bent to touch down, she opened her mouth, and, looking into the face of a man, lying chained upon the charred earth, with eyes endless and clear and the color of amethyst, she sang a soft sound to him. He leaned upward to hear it, to take it in, and he smiled and looked above.

Above.

Into her soothing visage.

And beyond.

To a figure, descending, arms spread, outreached, slowly, slowly, gliding down from the heavens in a blinding light.

And then, there was a whiplash of lightning and the woman and the figure soared upwards and the skies closed and crackled with innumerable colors, and the man felt himself drawn up with them, after them, into a whirlpool which shook him and whipped him about, until blackness enveloped him.

Silence.

Stillness.

And finally, light.

As Balthazar awoke to the gentle sound of the night fading to early day, the insects cooing to the coming warmth.

He looked at his comrades, asleep in their tent, then gingerly rose and walked outside.

He lifted his hands and placed them in a pattern across the fleeing night sky, framing a singular constellation. Then he brought them down, slowly, down across the horizon, as he watched a peculiar static play out, moving, slowly along its spine.

"Did you have the dream as well?"

Balthazar turned to Melchior behind him.

"Yes."

"Then we have been warned, to leave by way we have never seen, to flee from the dangers of this land," Melchior said.

They looked upon the horizon.

"Or to stay, and find a different path," Balthazar said.

They watched as the figures began to emerge, advancing across the distance, like a spreading stain.

Six, much larger than the rest, on animals twice the size of all others, leading the way.

And behind them, an army of men on horseback, their armor glimmering in the emerging day's sun.

Then, oddly, with a sizeable chunk of the array of horses and men continuing on towards the three Magi, another larger group broke off, heading into the desert, to parts unknown.

"Curious," Melchior said.

"Ominous," Balthazar said.

"What do we do?" Gaspar asked, now behind them, drawing his sword. "Herod is a paranoid and tempestuous ruler. He will no doubt think darkly of us returning to his kingdom. Especially past his own loaded farewell after our initial visit to him."

"He will likely suspect us to be spies at best," Melchior said.

"And at worst?" Gaspar said.

"Let him suspect what he will," Balthazar said. "It is truth. And the time for façade has passed."

Balthazar motioned and the hulking Gaspar sheathed his weapon.

"We have two choices: Attempt to flee, and be driven farther from that which we are here to protect, or, allow them to take us, to guide us to our new pathway," Balthazar said, "and remember, an illness does its most damage from the inside."

TWELVE

As the day crackled before him, the Arimathean leaned back in his chair, hoping to drown the incessant throbbing in his head. Perched against his home, he drank deeply and watched as his neighbor, James, and James' oldest grandson, Simon, worked in the shop next door, amiably chatting between themselves.

A skein of women cloaked in black turgidly wandered through the main street. Leaving a long, dusty trail pocked by their darkened dirt tears behind them, the shrouded, sobbing tribe of mourners found their path unexpectedly ended by a welcome ray of joy.

A baby boy.

James grinned as he watched his toddler grandson stop and giggle at the women in their funeral gear, causing them to pause and, perhaps in surprise, perhaps with the unexpected break in their suffering, begin laughing over their tears.

For a moment, they gathered to consider the boy, and then, with a few whispered words between them, they stopped to watch, happily, as he reached down to grab a small shock of lamb's wool and hand it to them, proudly sharing his most prized possession.

The women, obviously touched, looked over the toy and then handed it back to him, continuing on, still mourning, but heartened and hopeful.

The boy waddled about, bobbing and weaving to the song on his mother's voice as she tended to her garden. He wandered to her side, gleefully cradling the worn, dusty toy. It would seem little more than a rag to most, something to be used and discarded, but to the child tossing and chasing it about it seemed an incredible treasure, and to Simon, little older than the toddler himself, it was likewise invaluable to witness.

The tiny boy, James' youngest grandson, Jude, had been a terrific diversion to a long day of work. The boy's laughter and smiles as he wandered in and out of the shade of his home, playing various games with his small baubles and cloths, brightened James' mind and lightened his back as he dedicated his time to more arduous tasks.

The day was mercifully winding down, the relentless sun giving way to cool breezes and the promise of a quilt of stars. James wiped the sweat dripping off his graying locks across his leathered face. He stretched, still chuckling at the little boy waddling about just a few feet away from his proud mother, who pulled the day's laundry from the tree's branches shading their tiny home.

Simon groaned as he arched his back. His grandfather slapped his shoulder.

"You sound like me!" the older man said, helping Simon gather the day's labor to bring inside. "You are barely nine summers boy. Wait until you are…"

"Ninety nine summers?" Simon said, laughing.

"One-hundred and ninety-nine!" the older man said, posing robustly. "And still as strong as I was when I was your age! Stronger!"

"You will have to share your secrets with me, grandfather," Simon said as he lifted the last box. "Actually, I should say all your secrets."

"In time, my boy, in time."

In truth, his grandfather, and his father, also named James, had already shared much, very much, with Simon. The boy already felt well on his way to manhood given the training his grandfather had imparted. But this was why his father had left Simon behind, as he traveled, to have his grandfather instruct him in the same trades and sacred scrolls as his father, while Simon and James the Elder took care of the family during the father's occupational journeys.

Days and nights were dedicated to their crafts, carpentry and the secret arts. Simon was an eager and attentive learner, hungering for his grandfather's approval. A smile. A pat on the head. And, most importantly, the look of silent pride on his face, that he was living in line with his ancestors, and that, somewhere, they too were proud.

Simon moved the last of their day's work into their home and his grandfather put his hand on his shoulder, then around it, kissing the top of his head and smiling. Simon looked up at him and beamed.

"Time for dinner," his grandfather said. "I suspect we have both earned hearty appetites this evening."

Simon nodded and took another look at the toddler, trundling back to his mother, who was breaking off small, gnarled chunks of bread for the boy.

"Grandfather, can I?"

The older man looked at the woman and child.

"Of course."

As his grandfather made his way inside, Simon walked briskly to his mother and brother, kissing and hugging the woman, and began playing with the toddler. The woman smiled glowingly. Her husband, James, had left months before, but had yet to return. Rumors had flown that he was dead, or a prisoner, but she refused to deny hope, refused to believe that her husband was gone, hoping that he would someday return.

As the days grew longer, though, Simon and his grandfather began to take the long-gone father's responsibility as their own. It was well understood by any of the rougher elements of the town who would harbor untoward thoughts that the mother and infant child were under the wing of the robust older man and his strapping young son. And as those men of ill means had seen and heard, also beneath that wing was a claw ready to strike brutally in retaliation.

Unbeknownst to all, the Arimathean had begun to take an interest in them as well. Not so much romantic or paternal in regard to the woman and child, but curious and honorable. He knew of the family's place within the order of his own long-abandoned secret sect and respected their dedication, their devotion not only to its honorable tenets but also to the protection of those who needed it. That steadfast faith and adherence to the old ways, exhibited by the grandfather and being passed to the boy, intrigued the Arimathean and stirred his admiration.

And, perhaps, in a way, however insignificant and small, the Arimathean's discreet interest in looking over them all was an attempt to fill a void in his heart, to help heal a distant scar.

As the woman gathered a few meager items, Simon noticed the rest of their small village square winding down. The men shutting up shops, pulling their wares in, securing them for another day. The women collecting their children, making their way to the earthenware, working their alchemy with the scant delectables before them. Inside their humble dwellings, plates grew with food and fires began to light against the growing darkness. The din of the market grew low, then silent, and the melodies of the approaching dusk bled in over the cozy buzz of distant chatter inside glowing hearths.

Accompanied by . . . something unusual.

"Simon!" His grandfather called.

As Simon walked towards his house, he began to hear the noise, in the distance.

"It sounds like thunder," his grandfather called. "We had better prepare for the storm. Tell your mother and brother to come inside."

"Yes, grandfather."

Simon looked off into the distance. The sound grew louder, heavier, yet more insistent. He watched the horizon. Squinted at the strange oscillation above the ground, looking like flames of earth whipping towards the sky.

The Arimathean had noticed it as well.

"An unusual storm looming," the Arimathean said to the boy, pointing into a dark and growing cloud along the horizon.

"Yes," Simon said.

The Arimathean and boy stood silently, eyeing the sinister line seeping across the desert, the pyre of dirt rising high around it, as the sun set low and the darkness caved in behind it.

"Get your grandfather," the Arimathean said.

Simon ran into the house.

Seconds later, his grandfather bounded out with him, watching the desert expanse. He stretched out his palms and placed his fingers across the earth and sky before them, measuring.

"We must hurry," the old man said. "Quickly."

Simon ran to get his mother and brother, leading them to a strange outcropping of rocks just outside the back of their home, and with a few brisk movements, opened an entryway and hustled the woman and child inside.

"Stay here, you will be safe," he said.

He moved to quickly close the portal and replace its disguise, but her hand caught him just before.

His warm, silver blue eyes looked deep into her wide green pools. "Do not worry," he said. "We will protect you."

"But who will protect you, my son?" she said, her voice breaking.

"I will come for you soon," the boy said, smiling as he shut the portal and rushed back to their home. His grandfather was inside, rustling about, opening secret passageways and hiding spots, retrieving some items, dispatching others into dark, clandestine portals beneath the modest domicile.

He emerged from the room below, grim yet possessed of an eerie calm, with a strange companion upon his arm.

A white owl, strikingly handsome, with a small scroll tied about its leg.

With a quick whistle, the old man released the bird into the sky and it soared away.

Simon and his grandfather watched it, a lone pure object of beauty disappearing into the gathering dark.

They heard the first screams on the edge of town and hurried, hurried to prepare as the wails and cries grew louder, nearer, faster.

Closer.

The Arimathean entered the doorway.

"What is the kid doing here? You know what looms ahead. Get him into hiding with the woman and child."

"That is not his place. He is the eldest. His place is here."

The older man looked at his grandson.

"But not by our side."

The Arimathean nodded.

The boy looked at his grandfather, crestfallen.

"Simon, I know you wish to, but, you know what you must do," his grandfather said, putting his hand on his shoulder, then grabbing him and hugging him tightly, then guiding him down the dusty carved stairway hidden beneath their home. "You must stand guard, with the sacred writings, and not leave your post, no matter what you may hear above."

"Grandfather!"

"Quickly!" the old man called out. "Close the door!"

The old man looked at Simon.

The boy's eyes welled with tears.

The old man smiled.

"I love you, Simon."

"I love you, baba."

The old man's eyes welled as he reached down and touched the boy's face, smiling at him, then pulling him close once more, before placing his hands on both the boy's shoulders.

With a heavy sigh, he looked into his grandson's face once more.

"If I do not see you in this life, I will see you in the next one. I promise," the older man said. "I love you."

James the Elder turned from Simon. The Arimathean looked away to the fury exploding outside, then he and the old man turned and pushed through the exit, pulling their swords from worn leather sheathes as they roared towards the sounds of chaos coming from the streets, cascading through their town.

Simon quickly pulled the door and its camouflage shut. He sealed and placed the scrolls and ornaments into the wall and pulled their own door and camouflage down upon them, ripped the rocks and sticks and clay and tossed dust from the ground into the air about the secret shelves and his place of hiding to give it the look and feel of abandonment, as if this were only a safe haven for the boy.

Just in case.

They found him.

He went to the door, as his grandfather had taught him, and looked at the many locks on it, thought of how his grandfather had sealed each one, over and over, told Simon, over and over, never to open them, never to leave if anything like this were to happen.

But now it was happening.

And as Simon heard the sounds of steel smashing against steel, each brutal crash a blessing, a forfeiture of a killing blow, and he heard the bellows, the screams and wails of slaughter, he struggled with his training, shaking, shaking in indecision.

Finally, in quick motions he slapped the locks shut, slid them tightly closed.

All but one.

He thought of his grandfather.

Looked at the lock.

Looked down at the sword at his belt.

The sword he had been given by his grandfather.

His baba.

The sword he had been trained so diligently to wield. But only in defense of his station, his grandfather said. A station he was drilled never to leave. Never.

He remembered those words his grandfather had told him, over and over again. Today, and in so many days passed.

"You will never lose me," he said, looking into Simon's eyes. "I will always be with you.

"And if I cannot see you in this life, I will see you in the next one."

Simon lifted his hands from his sword and put them to the steel of the last, largest lock, began to move it, shove it into position, shutting out the world.

And then he heard it.

A familiar sound.

Then another.

A baby's scream.

A mother's cry.

Steel on steel.

A horrifying cry.

And then, silence.

THIRTEEN

Servants bowed and gasped as The Six led the Magi, resplendent in the exotic accoutrements of royalty, into Herod's temple and up a long red carpet towards the throne.

Still sleeked in sweat and slipping a silken robe over his rounded form, Herod emerged from behind the folds of a golden skein of curtains flanking the throne and smiled when he saw the three before him.

"So nice of you to join us again," Herod said. "I take it your search for the new king has not yet been a fruitful one, judging by your surprisingly lengthy stay in my kingdom?"

"Actually, we were hoping to discover if you had made any new progress in your own search," Melchior said.

"Indeed," Herod said, lounging on the throne. "And I assume that is why you have so graciously agreed to retire to my palace once more in your long journey?"

The Magi were silent.

"You first came to me a moon ago, asking about a new king you had seen foretold in the stars," Herod said. "Have the heavens failed you?"

"The heavens are sometimes slow to unravel their tales," Balthazar said.

"Yes," Herod said. "And sometimes not at all."

Herod rose and descended from the throne, standing among the men, looking them over, slithering between them like a viper, waiting to strike.

"Or sometimes, the tales come not to those who expect them, but to those who seek to discover them."

Then he tipped his head back towards the throne and the curtains behind it, beckoning the three to join him.

"But where are my manners?" Herod said, extending his arms with mock courtesy. "You are noblemen, travelers from afar, and we must attend to your needs in a manner well deserved for such royal visitors to my kingdom."

He walked towards the curtains, inviting them in.

"Come."

The Magi followed, with The Six behind them a few paces.

Herod nodded and a pair of servants parted the curtains.

There, behind the throne, was a massive room saturated in rich shades of crimson, violet and gold. Upon the walls were written dark, devious looking runes, scarring the room in a strange tattoo. The space was illuminated by endless candles upon jagged stands of awkward and uneven heights, interspersed with hanging censers of pungent and heady incense.

A chorus of monks in black robes stood at the four corners of the room, three to each corner, emitting a low, otherworldly dirge. Another man, in an elaborate costume that melded the traits of a jackal and viper, walked slowly in a circle around the room, waving a golden scepter with a reptilian face. His head was covered by a bejeweled helmet with a matching demonic countenance that rippled blue fire as he waved the scepter. The man alternated unsettlingly between delicate whispers and guttural growls in an alien language.

In the middle of the room were all manner of white and purple silk pillows and beddings and writhing within their confines were dozens of naked bodies, in full throes of passion, bathed in sweat, cries and moans.

"Should you wish to partake?" Herod asked, motioning to the twisted, tawdry mess of limbs.

The Magi demurred.

"These are among my finest slaves, and nobles of the kingdom enjoying their pleasures," Herod said. "For why else do they exist, if not to please us?"

Herod looked upon the orgy with blazing eyes, licking his lips.

He turned to the Magi and, sotto voce, sneered, "I have told them that if they perform... admirably, they may be freed. And they may."

Herod smirked.

"Or may not."

Herod paused and looked the Magi over.

"You are certain you do not wish to join us?"

Their faces remained stoic.

The king looked back to The Six with a subtle nod.

"Or perhaps," Herod said to the Magi, "you require other sustenance?"

Herod led them on, through another thick curtain and into an adjoining room.

Within it, once more, were the runes, the illumination, the censers of incense and another priest in odd garb, chanting slowly as he circled.

But the room's center was dominated by a far different tableau.

A tremendous, smoking pit, hot bottomed with flame.

Rising from it were thick, jagged, irregular steel skewers, more than large enough to impale a man.

Herod gazed upon the Magi, then to the pit.

He breathed deeply and smiled.

Then he walked slowly back to the curtain between the two rooms, pulled it open slightly, looked upon the orgy and cackled demonically.

"First they shall feed our loins," Herod said, "and then, our gullets."

Herod grinned sardonically and looked at the three.

"And you shall join us."

Balthazar nodded slightly.

"We are honored by such an invitation, but must decline," Balthazar said. "It is not our custom to . . ."

Herod stopped him with a raised hand and a low chuckle that grew into a deep laugh.

"I did not invite you as guests," Herod said, "but as the main course."

Herod gestured to the Six.

"Take them!"

Melchior and Gaspar quickly drew their swords and knives and assumed a defensive position, but Balthazar only raised a long, thin hand and gave each of his companions a calm look.

The two men sheathed their weapons and the three surrendered quietly.

"Take them to the tower," Herod said. "I will summon them when the ritual fires have grown to welcome them."

He looked at the Magi and raised an eyebrow.

"And when our appetites have grown to accommodate them."

—

FOURTEEN

The darkness had not completely devoured the town. The charred, rusted sun's last rays dusted the rocky ground, tarred by the shadows dripped across them, but still allowing a dim light to loiter around the solemn streets.

Within the houses, however, a forlorn, funereal gray reigned.

The centurions, agile and huge, slathering and cackling like hyenas attacking their prey, savaged into the doors and windows, greeted by screams and muted sounds of struggle. Inevitably, pathetically, the cries would turn to bloody gurgles, the anemic torches would be extinguished, and the last horrifying sounds of the dead, dying and those wishing for death would ooze through the barren spaces that just hours earlier were bouncing with the sounds of play and banter.

Simon snapped free the last lock of his place of hiding and shoved open the door to growing darkness in his house, the sounds of battle molesting the once halcyon streets outside it. He shut the secret portal, threw hulks of debris and blankets over quickly to hide it and ran to his door, sword in hand, to see a group of men facing their last stand.

It was a sad spectacle, only a few townsmen attempting, valiantly but vainly, to fight off the centurions, who were using the remnants as little more than play at this point. The Romans' armor was slicked with the blood of good men slain, the steel exoskeletons gleaming in the fires licking through the streets with every deadly movement as they cut down the last spasms of resistance.

Simon looked for his grandfather but could not find him amidst the anarchy of bodies downed. Then he heard the baby's cry again, the cry that had drawn him out of hiding. He turned and as a thick black cloud parted with a rush of wind, he saw the lamb's wool rag toy in the road among a thick of odd, twisted shapes.

He ran toward it and snatched it from the dirt.

Holding it close to him, his eyes welled.

A burst of flame roared.

And behind him, he glimpsed a figure.

He turned to face it, and watched as the sword was swung, bearing down on his neck. Simon had little time to block or cushion the blow. Out of instinct, he jerked to lift his sword, and his movements caused him to trip over something in the road, sending him tumbling backwards as the metal sliced the air just above his head.

The centurion, not expecting to miss, found himself in an awkward lurch over Simon. Lunging forward at the off-balance warrior, Simon did not hesitate, burying his sword upward, as his grandfather had taught him, beneath the metal shell around the man's torso, and into his belly, twisting the sword and quickly removing it. The soldier struggled, fell to his knees, slowly raised his arm to strike again, to cut the boy down, but once more, Simon's movements were fast and liquid, slicing the soldier's throat in one clean motion.

The blood from the man's jugular sprayed into Simon's face, baptizing him and stunning him as he stopped for a moment, realizing what he had done.

For the first time.

He was not training. Not cutting a bag or a wooden dummy. But a man.

Taking a man's life.

He froze for a second, and then realized where he was, what he was doing, and how he had tripped and fallen.

Below him, motionless and mangled, were bodies.

Bodies of men and women he had just seen smiling and happy.

And one, one more familiar than the rest.

The body of his grandfather.

James the Elder.

The once-kind face of his beloved mentor.

His baba.

Forever frozen in agony.

His face broke in tears, but Simon had no time for grief. He was jarred alert by the squeal of a mother and child again. He followed the calls for pity and saw them being chased from a burning home, then falling, falling forward to the unforgiving, dusty ground.

His worst fears became realized.

It was them.

His mother.

His brother Jude.

Either their hiding place had been uncovered, or, most likely, they had left it, probably out of concern for Simon. Trying to find him. Protect him.

Their eyes met.

His in shock and sorrow.

Hers in surprise and fear.

And then, the mother's eyes, those once-kind green pools, rolled white. That once-smiling mouth gagged red as she collapsed, under the weight of the gaping wound he saw jaggedly smirking from her back, and the sadistic kick from a centurion forcing her to the dirt.

The Roman soldier, with a spiky black beard and red eyes scalding through his golden helmet, let out a cackle and heaved his blade over the baby boy, who lay crying and dazed on the ground where his mother had fallen.

Simon grabbed the sheath at his leg, the one his grandfather had given him, and in one motion sent two tiny, razor sharp shuriken stars into the centurion's face, blinding him and sending him tumbling backward, his head jerked back, exposing his neck. In another quicksilver move, Simon whipped two more into the Roman's jugular and the bearded man fell backwards, dead.

Simon looked to Jude. The toddler, wailing, oblivious, was no longer pointed towards his mother, but now his vision, clouded by tears and smoke, flung to the toy, which Simon had dropped in the chaos. The dirty treasure had blown towards the boy, and his little arms and legs teetered ambitiously to secure it.

The toddler grabbed for it, as another soldier appeared, a leering grin dripping from his face, over the infant.

Simon lunged forward for his brother as he heard the sound of metal scything through the oppressive humidity.

The soldier's sword thundered down!

Simon was able to grab the boy and hurtle away, falling hard to the ground, back first to protect the boy clutched to his chest. He turned, spun and rolled just in time to avoid death, as the soldier's sword clanged loudly about them, slamming into the rocky earth.

The boy shrieked, held tight in Simon's arms. They struggled to flee, but the boy's squirming made it impossible to once more agilely spin away from an attack.

The soldier raised his sword once more and brought it down upon them both.

There was no way to escape it.

Simon held the boy tight to his chest and quickly muttered a solemn prayer. Just hoping they would arrive in a better place, a kinder place. The two of them, together. Brothers, side by side.

The blade whipped down, driven with animalistic bloodlust, with enough force to split both children in two.

But there, with a violent, muscular clash of steel, to block it, was the Arimathean.

The soldier's sword came down savagely, at an odd angle, careening off the edge of the Arimathean's sword and tearing a cruel swath across his face. It barely missed being a killing or maiming blow, but still sliced the skin, sprayed blood into the Arimathean's eyes and temporarily blinded him.

Simon watched as the Arimathean ignored the red slash dripping down his cheek and with one swift, powerful move, impaled the soldier before him. The Arimathean's sword fired from his massive arm with such force that it tore through the Roman's armor as if it was little but silk.

Simon felt the frightened boy squirm, heard him scream. He sighed, joyous, through his own pain. The boy was alive. That was all that mattered.

A horseman bore down on them, about to crush them with a mace, but the Arimathean grabbed a discarded torch and waved his hand with the casual skill of a mage, and a burst of enchanted flame erupted from it, startling the soldier's steed. With a blindingly fast swing the Arimathean dislodged the soldier from his saddle; the man tumbled from its perch, disoriented as the Arimathean sent his sword screaming through the air and the soldier's head soon with it, splattering blood upon the ground.

But more horsemen advanced, swarming the Arimathean like angry wasps, raining steel through the air.

He used his magicks to create a wall of flame around him, charring a line of warriors and sending them howling away. However, it wasn't enough. More soldiers seeped towards him like a stain, their swords shrieking through the air. The Arimathean parried and swung, killing blow after killing blow, until he was eclipsed by an ever growing maw of centurions, closing about him.

Simon cowered, watched the frenzy, considered the scene before him, quickly breathed a prayer, thought about leaping into the fray, but reconsidered.

He wished he could help, but realized he had no choice.

Simon wiped his vision of blood and dirt and he ran, holding the small boy, squidging in his arms, kicking and screaming. He heard another horseman turn awkwardly to bear down upon them, leaping from his steed to capture the boys on foot as they scrambled through the debris.

He heard the soldier's lunges rip through the dirt of his shadow, felt the weight of the Roman's sword sever the air just behind him, barely nicking his back and drawing blood once more. For a half-second after the metal sliced through Simon's skin and muscle, his left arm gave way and the squirming boy came loose, but his right arm held fast and his brother remained, as they jumped through a doorway just as the full force of the sword shattered the hardened clay and rock above it.

The ensuing mess tumbled a pool of rubble onto the path and caused the man to slip and fall, allowing Simon and the boy to escape, escape through the small hovel and into the back yard, darting through the maze of spaces too small for the soldier to make, into the tight paths between buildings, through cracks and crevices and finally into a yard festooned with freshly cleaned robes, hanging to dry.

Through the haze of his wounded vision, his eyes burning from smoke and sweat and blood, his head throbbing from his tumbles to the hard ground, Simon grabbed a robe and staunched the flow of blood from his back. He wrapped it quickly around him, looked about, and grabbed another smaller vestment.

"I am sorry, little one," Simon said, sighing. He placed the wadded up garment over the mouth of his brother and covered it with his hand, to silence the infant, which caused the boy to struggle all the more. "You will thank me for it later, for being around to thank me for it later."

Simon took a few seconds and realized where he was, then went back through an alternate path, slowly traversing the maze of robes hanging about him, acting as a crude subterfuge, checking to make sure he wasn't leaving a trail of blood behind, until he and the child got to a small, ramshackle edifice that looked like it hadn't been inhabited for years.

He looked around.

Nothing.

Nothing but the wind on the robes.

Nothing.

But out of the corner of his eye, a shadow.

Then a wisp of dust kicked forward.

He heard the clank of centurions' armor. The steel being slung high.

Seconds.

He had seconds.

He turned to see the sword raised, and as it came down in a hearty swath, Simon dropped quickly into a cat-like crouch, dodging the attack. Then in one liquid movement, his arms still tight around the child, Simon whirled and scissored his legs hard across the exposed flank of the centurion's knee. He knocked the soldier to the ground, the Roman's jagged sword impaled in the wall of the edifice behind him, carried by the force of his missed would-be death blow.

Simon took no mercy on the fallen. He let go of his brother, setting him on the ground, and in a blur, as the soldier remained dazed, Simon sprung back up, lifted his right leg sharply above the prone man's neck and brought his foot down, as he had been taught, with all the force he could muster, decimating the soldier's windpipe and snapping his spine.

Then, quickly, he picked up his brother, ran around the back of another house, removed a large shank of brush and debris, and, just as he heard the clank of other centurions' armor crashing towards the edifice they had left, he lowered himself into a hole he had once dug and replaced its camouflage.

Once inside, he climbed down into the catacombs beneath the city. In more carefree days he had spent hours exploring them, learning their expanses and odd caprices. Now, his knowledge was a matter of life and death, for him and his brother.

He fled far, far down, through paths that only he knew, to a dark recess near a small stream. He cleaned his wounds, treated them with fungi and arcane plants growing below that he had been taught about, fed himself and the child with wild flora, waited what seemed like days, then walked to another exit and emerged just outside the town, in the dark of the desert.

With the child sleeping in his arms, he stared glumly at the town, under a ghastly plague of smoke from fires left burning in the long-gone marauders' wake. His chest bobbled and quaked and his eyes damped. He swallowed hard, then sighed and looked back into the desert beyond, and into the night sky.

There, pale but steadfast, was the sign. The sentinel of his faith.

Stoic and simple, burning bright, just below the moon, just above two lesser orbs glowing beneath it.

The star.

The star his grandfather had showed him, told him about.

The star that every night, they looked to as they traded stories on their night walks.

Walks he would take no more.

With a man he would never see again.

He looked to the star, with tears in his eyes, then looked down at the boy, the infant's blissfully oblivious, beautifully sleeping face, and kissed his brother's cheek.

Then, with nothing but hope, he returned to the town, to embrace or bury and mourn his grandfather, his mother, the Arimathean, and the rest.

To try to survive. To try to get by. To try to be strong.

To live alone with his younger brother, in hiding, on the supplies he and his grandfather had stocked for this circumstance. To recapture the sacred texts his grandfather had hidden, resume his training, begin the training of the boy, and to wait until their father, hopefully, returned.

Wait, wait and watch as the star bloomed brighter, brighter, seemingly closer, closer. Watch as it grew as his hope would have to, for a future better than the present immediately betrayed before him.

But in the distance, he could hear them.

The stampeding tide of murderers.

Beating.

Pounding.

Stabbing away.

Echoes haunting his mind?

Or the awful howls of the bloodthirsty pack far in the distance, hungrily eyeing the meat of a new array of victims.

FIFTEEN

All of their humble, threadbare possessions were strapped to the back of their steeds, hanging down the sides. The belongings positioned to make the ride as comfortable as possible for the most precious cargo among them all, Mary and her unborn child. With the silence of the night pulling back to the bustle of a new day, Joseph and Mary prepared to leave. They thanked their hosts for the evening, the first stop upon their trek, and once more set out, ostensibly to travel to the place of their own births.

Or at least the birthplace of those whose names were on their forged identities, as had been secured by Joseph, through the secret hand.

It would be best to feign compliance with the decree, Joseph and the confidantes of Mary's family had agreed. The reaction to it among their populace was unpopular at best, virulent and violent against Rome and its imposition at its apex. But given the circumstances, there was wisdom only in acquiescence, at least upon the surface.

The men of the secret order had suspected the census had an ulterior motive, particularly one conjunctive with the order of the stars, the ancient prophecies, the frequency with which prophets seemed to have been foretold as arriving in this time. The elders among them had passed down a suspicion of any survey or surveillance, for they had a checkered history at best. Most had often been little but a charade, a veiled way of locating, profiling and often detaining those the Empire had deemed a threat.

How best for those in power to deal with those who had been foreseen as having the potential to unseat them?

To identify them, locate them, then monitor them.

And, if needed, destroy them.

Hence, a census.

And so Mary and Joseph began a path to a destination unseen to all but themselves. In full sight of those in authority, albeit under the cover of assumed names.

They knew this would buy them time, but it would guarantee nothing, and how much time would not be known, hopefully until it was too late for it to matter, hopefully until after they were safe.

As they rode the barren trails, Joseph contemplated the circumstances that had brought him to this point.

He had been raised in the house of David, trained in the ways of the silent hand, taught in the scrolls and the arts of combat, and, through his ancestors, had been prepared for precisely such a moment as this.

But he had never sought it.

Even from a young age, he found himself shying from what he felt to be futile gestures of war. Violence begetting violence. Giving those in power reason to slather their opposition, however justified, or not, in enemies' garb.

"People use force because they feel it their only recourse when force is used upon them," Joseph once said to Mary's father, as they had discussed the fomenting of another rebellion against the Empire. "More people would eschew it, would do the right thing, would take more peaceful means of change, if they weren't afraid to do so, if they did not believe their actions would be futile."

"Most men are evil, evil at heart," Mary's father had scoffed. "They only understand and respond to force."

"Men are not intrinsically evil," Joseph replied. "Everyone is born innocent. All are good. It is the world that makes them otherwise. So if you can change the world, you can change the hearts of mankind."

Mary's father merely smiled and shook his head in doubt.

But he would later discover that Mary, who had been eavesdropping, felt in her chest a flutter, and in Joseph's words realized a kindred spirit.

He had seen battle, perhaps more than he would ever say. However, he was unlike so many of those that had. He was far more contemplative and distant, preferring solitude and solace to the fields of war and the machinations of conflict against the Empire, overthrowing the status quo.

"Men of great power, regardless of religion or culture or breeding, always find the lust for greater power to be their ultimate master," Mary's father once said to him.

"All the more reason, then, to eschew all labels of such and recognize where the true divisions between us lie," Joseph replied, "and therefore see how to potentially bridge them."

His younger years had been those of rebellion and idealism, following in the grooved paths of those heroes before him, alive only in memories, soaring and perfect in tales told, no longer confined to the inconvenient questions posed by the flesh.

He followed the momentum of those about him, the youth whose breasts burned wild and feral, fired by glories promised, heeded by the cries and delusions of their own imaginations, the futures they hoped they were born to embody. They bled away the last days of their childhoods and the explosive initial harvesting of their adult lives battling the occupiers and their traitorous lackeys, striving, they thought, to help the poor and starving, the sick and oppressed.

But it became all too much.

And all too little.

He felt himself drowning, cynical, slowly eclipsed, tarred as a man working in the mines, searching for precious stones but all too often finding himself tired and ragged, having exhausted himself for little more than a maintenance of the status quo, at best making strained moves forward, however slight.

He sought to leave a life of turbulence and uncertainty, of action and sub rosa peregrinations, to follow a simple life of a carpenter. Best to use his skills to build something tangible, he thought, something which would hold up over time, would offer a visible betterment of someone's life.

"Oftentimes it is the simple things which make the most lasting impact," he once said to Mary. "If you can change one person's life in a small way, perhaps they will help change another's and so it will continue, as a ripple on the sea from one pebble, building to a wave. There are more good people than bad, far more, but they need to realize that and change the world by not allowing those in power to corrupt them, by creating their own world aside from the one which would taint and stain them, and, by example, drawing others in. If they are able to do that, to create a new world, a world of honesty and good, which were to rise to the highest power, completely independent of the existing corrupt structure, then those of evil means would have no sway over them."

He remembered, still, the day he set his sword aside.

Remembered hearing the wails of the mourning still in his ears, haunting his memories, the women of his town, lamenting their slaughtered sons, their husbands, their brothers.

He remembered looking upon his steel, and thought upon loved ones in other towns, ones who had been painted as enemies, but were soldiers, like he and his compatriots, swayed by and following the orders of those who pushed them forward to die in passion for a cause, while they remained safely behind.

He thought of those soldiers and their families, mourning, wailing the same way.

Thought of mothers who would never hold their sons again.

Thought of children who would grow to adulthood having never seen the smiling faces of their fathers.

That day he set down his sword, and, remembering the words of the prophet Isaiah, began smashing it against a massive rock, beating it into a plowshare. Then, he let it fall, cleaving to the soil, vowing never to lift it again.

A vow which he had held and kept to this day.

He wandered, plying his wares, helping to construct and instruct, and was weary and beyond hope of finding anything but solitude as a beacon when he strode into Mary's village.

Taking odd jobs among the people, he strove to find peace, and, perhaps, at long last, some certainty, a place to call home.

Mary's father, a good man, hired him soon after his arrival.

When he first met Mary, he was immediately struck by her, her beauty and her caring, her innocence and her way of embracing the world about her. He had been so careful, so suspicious and tentative, raised to be wizened and severe, distant and contemplative, and at first he was taken aback and, to his shame, almost distrustful of her openness and generosity.

But he soon found it to be genuine, a panacea to his world-weary demeanor and a kindling to his burgeoning love and affection for her.

Joseph looked upon her, so unlike so many others he had encountered. He had been watching her from afar, enamored but uncertain of her, insecure of the age between them, respectful of her father and not wanting to be untoward.

However, the more he watched her, the more he saw the way she played, she taught, she cared for, the children about her.

The more his heart began to thaw, to believe in her sincerity, the wonder inside her.

And slowly, slowly, he fell in love.

It took quite a while for him to overcome a feeling he was unworthy of one so fragile and tender, one so rare and beautiful. He felt himself too much a charred and scuffed emerald for her purity. But he was too drawn to her, felt too strong a connection not to brave his insecurity.

He approached her in a humble manner, building an aviary for the wounded birds to which she tended. Soon, their conversation became more frequent, elaborate. He did not trust, hesitated for a long while as he spent time around and with her, studied her, and, eventually, allowed her into his confidence, and, his heart.

It was a quick attraction but a slow courtship, a friendship of sorts that was fast to blossom into a deep and abiding love that neither wanted to acknowledge for fear of appearing improper, but both could tell was present.

Before long, he could not imagine his life without her.

And all the more, he felt almost an obligation to her, to be with her, to protect her. He was so amazed and enthralled by her, by the fact that the world could be home to someone like her. He wished more deeply than anything that she could remain so, remain pure and innocent, a bastion of that which the world should be, rather than yet another example of what it settled upon being.

And, true to her own words of fate and destiny, in some way, he realized everything he had experienced had led him to her, to the point where he was meant to not only be with her, but was rare in his respect and admiration of her and his desire for her to retain that lightness of being.

Upon first hearing of her impending pregnancy, knowing they had refrained from union, his soul cracked and shattered. His cynicism and the pessimism of the world he had experienced gained the better of him. He had seen this before, men of character, particularly older men, cuckolded by younger women lacking thereof, looking for someone of substance to atone for their indiscretions, for their wide-eyed lies.

But he was still a man of compassion, and she seemed so sincere and beyond reproach that, even while half of him cursed the other for being naïve and stupid, he felt too much to cast her aside to suffer the fate of an adulteress.

So, rather than publicly humiliating her, he suggested a slow, subtle break and ending of their engagement.

Her reaction was not what he expected.

Her tears, her words, sought to sway him, and forced him into uncertainty, made him promise to reconsider. He consulted her father, her mother, and they believed her to be too kind, too pure, to stray. However, they likewise believed that her condition may have been an unintended one, and despite her mistreatment, her tender way could be manipulated by one who feared for his life, who feared for the fate deserved for a wicked deed performed.

They had resolved to find the one who had forced himself upon her, and mete appropriate punishment, but do so without her knowledge, to retain her grace and innocence.

However, that same night they had consulted and plotted, Joseph, and Mary's parents, not only reconsidered their plan, but changed their beliefs entirely.

The visions, the words, Joseph experienced in dream, not only convinced him of Mary's honesty and sincerity in regard to their situation, but only reinforced his belief that he, alone, had been meant to be with her, had been meant to be in this situation, to protect and love her, and the son which they would bring into the world. Her parents, having similar messages delivered in dream, thought the same.

"Who are we to say we believe in the scriptures and then, when their miracles are brought to our lives, deny that same faith in them?" Joseph said.

How odd, he thought, that his bloodline and training had brought him to such a point. That he had been brought to this fate at the precise moment in which he had fled from any want of responsibility for anything close to a commitment such as this.

But likewise, how ironic that it was his bloodline and training that would have prepared him for this. How ironic that such a potentially violent passing through this time, that they and so many others would have to endure, the mindless purges and bloodshed, the wanton fist of power seeking to crush them, could lead to hope, hope for a more peaceful future, just as he had almost given up on one.

Joseph looked upon his wife and smiled.

At the very least, he thought, regardless of any scriptures or prophecies, the world was better for her being in it, and would be better, all the more, for a child who would reflect her kindness and love onto the world.

And for that, he would give his life.

For her.

For their son.

"What were you thinking?" she asked him.

"Of you," he said, kissing her and holding her hand. "Always."

As the sun rose higher, slowly higher, other travelers began to join them along the dusty, beaten paths between cities and settlings, villages and hovels.

Some made conversation, most remained silent, making the trip all the more steady and, in its own way, serene.

But also making it all the more chilling when the first sounds were heard.

Initially, it appeared to be thunder, a droning wave far in the distance. But the skies were bright, clean and blue, with barely the faintest wisps of clouds lonely and wandering above on light winds.

Then the rumbling grew louder, louder, and Joseph recognized the sound, one he had heard, and rued, so many times in the past.

He turned to his wife, grasping her hand and looking urgently into her eyes.

"We have to go."

SIXTEEN

Twisted among the dead and dying, his blood mingling with theirs in the dust and sand, the Arimathean drifted just beyond consciousness.

The wound on the back of his skull had not been fatal, but a fortunate irony, the result of an errant sword handle, knocking him out.

The Arimathean had cleaved his way through a thick cadre of soldiers, leaving their bodies strewn about his, their horses fled and frightened. He had but one more remaining, a tremendous warrior who had battled him feverishly.

He had finally found his way through the soldier's formidable defenses and buried his sword deep into the soldier's chest just as the centurion's arm violently jerked forward in death throes, hurtling the warrior's sword handle down heavily upon the back of the Arimathean's head. It bashed the Arimathean unconscious and propelled the dead man's body onto him. Since the ensuing throng of Romans inspecting the ruins thought the Arimathean's prone body a dismembered corpse, his bloody face barely visible under the huge fallen soldier, it rendered him immune to the predators' final lootings and defilements.

And so his body remained, untouched, abandoned, amidst the dead, scorched under the merciless sun.

As his mind lofted slowly between light and dark, he thought of the mother and child, of the boy, and hoped they had somehow survived.

Hoped and prayed they had not met the same fate as his family.

Unheeded, unwanted, his mind shocked back years earlier.

To another quest.

Another purge.

He had left. Left his family behind. Gone with the Magi to save the lives of another. Another family. Another child.

A boy named John.

The king had wanted him dead. The oracles had foretold his rise, his power, his ascension as a great leader of men. One who would stand apart, an iconoclast.

A threat.

And so it was the mission of the Magi and the Arimathean to find the boy, find his parents, and hide them away, ensconce them in the Magi's hidden web of secret societies, clandestine realms, keep them invisible and anonymous until the right time for their emergence.

The Arimathean had left. Left with the Magi. To do the work of God, or at least, the work he was told was that of God.

He left not knowing the lengths to which Herod would go.

He left his family behind.

His wife.

His sons.

His daughter.

Left them in the protection of his brother and the priests, the holy warriors who had helped keep him sharp in the arts of war, after he had descended from the Glowing City.

Taking the boy, John, and his parents, from the town, they disappeared into the desert, to better cast their spells within the void of the elements under the massive firmament and confuse Herod's oracles, until the heavens moved and the stars no longer betrayed them.

By that point they would be gone, on to their clandestine destination.

Safe.

They had found it odd, the Magi, how easily the trek was made, away, away, to safety. They had figured that at some point, perhaps, Herod's oracles would piece together what they had done and they would have to battle their way to their destination. They were pleased and surprised when they had not.

Little suspecting the real reason.

Only discovering it upon their return to the town of the Arimathean.

That Herod had figured he had succeeded in eliminating the boy.

Because he had destroyed so many others.

The few survivors who were left alive to tell the tale said they had never seen anything like it.

So savage.

Relentless.

Unstoppable.

The townspeople had put up a valiant fight, battled long and mightily against the odds, against the numbers. But in the end it was too much to survive. Too much to survive the blood-soaked armies of Herodius the Wicked.

So perverse and demonic was the attack and its aftermath that the few survivors were soon driven to madness and suicide, unable to escape the unhealable wounds carved in their memories.

Those bodies that were left unburned in town were mostly beyond recognition. Horribly defiled. Most half-eaten. Piles of flesh that had once been loved and loving human beings.

That had once been mothers and sons. Daughters.
Brothers.

Who had held.

Hugged.

Kissed.

Loved.

Played and laughed and lived.

No more.

The last image from his former home, the last he carried
with him as he left, the final wound burned into the
Arimathean's brain, was the sight of a child's security blanket,
rent and ripped asunder, stained and bloody, mockingly drifting
in on a lonely wind over the barren ground.

He remembered it wafting over to him, almost as if
following him, grasped upon him, being stained by his tears
falling to the ground.

Remembered it clinging to him, as if it had a mind of its
own, as he fell to his knees in the dirt.

Embracing him, like a small child.

Welcoming him home.

Begging him not to leave again.

Not to leave.

Not to leave.

Please.

But it was too late.

Too late.

Too late.

He remembered it.

Its feel.

Its scent.

Its scars. Its blood.

He remembered.

And his soul began to blaze again.

To burn. Burn. With a vicious rage. An unquenchable thirst. An insatiable need.

For steel.

For blood.

For revenge.

And so, with an explosion of will, he heaved himself up through the fires of memory and back, back to the killing grounds, under the sun scalding crimson and the spare, violet clouds that scratched the sky with the swirling chaos of a burning scar.

He thrust himself up, pushed his body through the rubble, through the bleeding, lifeless heaps of flesh that had fallen upon him, the men whose lives he had taken.

And he hurled them aside with spite and disregard, clenched his teeth and defied his pain, slunk to shelter, to tend his wounds, before leaving, to inflict that same deadly fate upon others.

SEVENTEEN

They cascaded upon the city like locusts, a swarm of centurions unlike the tiny dirt town had ever seen before. They cleaved through with zeal and purpose, raising dire clouds of dust blooming at the heels of their steeds, and when they leapt from the beasts they pocked the earth in steel-enforced sandals. They were men of unholy hungers, eyes glaring, teeth bared in evil grins, swords flashing.

The soldiers made quick work of the small series of primitive dwellings, easily shoving through the feeble resistance offered by doors or barriers or the men who dared to stand against them.

The sounds of steel slashing through the air were broken by the sickening chunk of metal eating flesh, the dull sticky thump of blades breaking bones, and always accompanied by the wails, the heartbreaking cries of the women, their last calls for mercy, unheeded.

The slaughter complete, the thunderous sound began again, as horses and men smashed over the ground, over the road, onto the next city, leaving behind moaning and lamentation in their wake.

When a sufficient amount of time had passed, the old man in the odd curio shop off a darkened side street, with the occult symbol upon his sign, emerged from his hiding, shambled back into a corner, behind a worn, dusty pile of rugs, beneath a decrepit shelf of books, and kicked the floor three times in a rhythmic pattern.

Three seconds later, the floor opened, a secret passageway, and from a hidden room beneath the shop, Joseph and Mary emerged.

"They are gone?" Joseph asked.

"Just a few moments ago the town went silent but for the sounds of mourning," the old man said. "It appears safe. However, there may be a few stragglers left behind, the usual vampires out to rape and pillage what they can to fatten their pockets and slake their lusts."

"We will be careful."

"Please do, my friends. Be wary. And God bless you and be with you."

"Thank you," Mary said. "So He shall be."

They accompanied the man around the side of his building to where their horses were hidden and continued their journey, careful in following the path mapped out before them, sadly traversing through the fields of cries and moans.

"The babies!" one old woman slurred and slumped about the street before crashing sadly against Joseph's steed, taking hold and not letting go. "They killed them all. The babies and their mothers. And all men who tried to stop them. Gone! Gone!"

Joseph descended from his horse and held her close, allowed her to extinguish her tears against him, her hands clenching tight to his robes, her body jerking and quaking in sorrow, until she calmed, exhausted. He set her down, sat with her, and gently wiped her hair away from her face.

"I promise you, God will help you through this," Joseph said. "I promise. Have faith."

"I have nothing else," the woman said.

She began to cry again, and Joseph comforted her, putting his arm around her gently. She drained herself until she began to breathe heavily and slowly, calming. She sat still, looking up as Joseph rose, and managed a slight nod of appreciation to the man and woman before her. Joseph and Mary bid her well, and continued their journey.

It was a disgusting march through moans of agony, and wails of mourning, pleading that would have to be ignored, have to be passed by, have to be disregarded, so as to not betray their greater purpose, their larger destiny.

"I feel terrible not helping to ease their pain," Mary said.

"I do as well, but we cannot, as much as we would like," Joseph said. "Your safety, our diligence in keeping on, and keeping you and our son safe, is too great to sacrifice."

Mary sighed, but nodded, softly, in acquiescence.

Joseph's conscience stabbed at him, churning and biting up his insides, but he knew the importance of the task ahead. He watched Mary, could tell the strain upon her already, could tell she would be close to birth sooner than they thought. And he knew of the dangers they could face, the import of them making it safely to their destination in time. Far more than his wife, he knew of what they could face. He knew the wickedness of men, the obscenities of war.

Unbidden, Joseph's mind sifted through similar scenes he had encountered.

He had never found the taste for battle. Unlike so many of his brethren, who had found its justification in the passion of their cause, as he saw more and more fighting, he only saw more and more suffering.

Joseph remembered one of the first towns he had encountered when he had abandoned his sword.

He had taken up as a stonemason's apprentice, and among his flock was a boy, a boy who showed an amazing proclivity for creation, for astounding sculpture and stonework, who brought otherworldly beauty from previously barren, nondescript slabs of earth.

Who had been raised, like him, to be a warrior.

The boy had beamed with pride as his family had tearfully accompanied him through an elaborate and amazing ceremony marking his entrance into adulthood, culminating in his acceptance of his own steel, his own place, among the men as they went forward to the battlefield.

Joseph recalled it was not so far before that the boy had been running amok, playing games and laughing, darting behind walls and ferreting his way between trees in mock tableaus of conflict, always finding his way to blessed victory.

"He will make a great champion for the cause, a great hero," the stonemason marveled at the young man.

Joseph offered little but a tacit nod, but his heart worried for the boy.

He remembered shaking the boy's hand in farewell, holding it tightly, offering a prayer for his safety, hoping for some salvation for him, the night before he went to war.

"You should be praying for those I will face," the boy scoffed, with a smirk.

And he rode off with the men, disappearing into the horizon, as those left behind returned to their lives, the boy becoming little more than a story, words passed between them, his presence no more.

It was less than a week on the true fields of battle that his body was brought back, limp and pale, incomplete.

Joseph was one of the men entrusted with its delivery. The once-spotless, smoothed pond stone skin of the heralded youth was nothing but a mangled lump of sallow, lifeless flesh. The once-brown sparkling eyes were not even milk white as they had been shortly after death, but were mostly hollowed, eaten by carrion. The once-smiling face, which had beamed with determination as he had marched away, was now cold and ashen gray. The skinny, lithe body, which had darted between the trees, was useless and broken, great heaves carved from it, leaving foul-smelling chunks that still seeped stains, ugly and ominous, through the shrouds placed over them.

Joseph had carried the dead many times before, but none had been so young, none had had such resonance for him. None had seemed so senseless, so brutal, so wasted.

The boy's mother thrashed and wept over his grave, her blackened robes stained all the darker by her relentless tears. The children of the town were solemn, half exploded in sobbing, the other half stunned silent and fearful, not only for their friend's passing, but for their own, possible fate, to befall them in just a few years beyond, just a moment past their once blessed childhood.

The fields of play remained fallow for long days after that.

And even beyond, for a considerable time, there were few games which attempted to echo the cries of war.

And yet, there were no tears shed by the ostensible leaders of the movement, of the city.

The men who had sent the boy to his death.

Only solemn words, dry eyes, doleful speeches which perversely utilized the young man's demise as a prompting for more, more conflict, more war, more boys like him being marched off to the slaughter.

And all while these same men, the elders, the men of wealth and power, would make the decisions to do so, to send them off, while never advancing towards the field themselves.

Heaven, they would speak of.

Heaven.

These warriors' final reward.

Their final resting place, for their valor, the place they had been promised.

Peace. Harmony. Happiness. All guaranteed.

In exchange for their peace, their happiness, their lives, the certainty of the rewards of this world.

Exchanging that certitude, those tangible goals in this life, for the promise of those in another, beyond, which they could only experience by sacrificing the joys of this one.

It was a savage irony, one which left Joseph perplexed and uncertain, distant and cold to its ways.

Joseph had been raised to regard the elders with respect. But he had grown to recognize that true respect can only be earned through actions, not imparted by words.

He looked upon the elders, heard their talk of heaven, their words spoken from a safe distance, which would guarantee them little chance of finding it any time soon.

"Heaven, heaven, heaven," the boy's mother said, through a tear-soaked scowl. "What do any of these parasites know of heaven? They sent my boy to die for their war, while they retreat from the battles of their own creation! Heaven. They talk of the riches of heaven while filling their pockets on earth. A camel would sooner find its way through the eye of a needle than these men would find their way into heaven!"

Joseph had held her, consoled her. He remembered the boy, hoped he had found peace, hoped he had found heaven. And that night, he had packed up his meager belongings and readied himself to leave, bidding farewell to his friends.

He had hoped he would never feel that same way again.

He had hoped.

They were almost to the end of the town when they walked by a pathetic, garbage and feces strewn alleyway, a receptacle, a dumping place for the trash of the city, when they heard the cries, the begging for mercy, for help.

They tried to pass by, but when they did, they were seen by the fallen, and the cries became all the more desperate.

"Please! Please! Help me! Help me!"

"No! No! I'm only a girl! Help! Please!"

Joseph knew his mission. He knew what he needed to do. But he could not. He could not bear to hear her gut-wrenching screams. He turned his head and saw a horrible sight.

Four soldiers had cornered a small girl, a girl who couldn't have been more than seven or eight years old. In the midst of the garbage and dirt and feces, they had obviously been playing a grotesque game of cat and mouse with her, battering her about, taunting and teasing and beating her, until now, until their disgusting denouement, in which they had torn all but the bare scraps of clothing from her and were about to take her final dignity.

Joseph stopped, looked at Mary, and looked at the men.

The girl's eyes met his.

"Please! Please! Help me! Please! I am only a girl!"

One of the soldiers brought a heavy, gloved hand down upon the side of her face, knocking her into a morass of garbage and filth upon the ground.

"You are a sorceress and a whore!" he said, with a devious smile. "And you will be treated as such."

The girl lifted her head and stared pleadingly at Joseph and Mary.

"Please . . ."

Tears ran down the girl's face.

Joseph descended from his horse and stepped forward.

"Stop!" Joseph said. "She is only a girl! What crime could she possibly commit, and how could it merit such punishment?"

The soldiers looked back. Joseph walked slowly, confidently, towards them.

"This doesn't concern you, citizen," a black-bearded centurion growled. "This girl has been branded a witch, a harlot, and we, the law of the Roman Empire, are dealing with her accordingly."

"But what of God's law?" Joseph asked.

"Please! Please!" the girl pleaded, down in the dirt, the first man about to be upon her now, loosening his belt.

The soldier glared at Joseph. "By the order of the Roman Empire, by the law of Herod, I command you to continue on," the soldier growled again.

At that point a second soldier walked towards to the first, looking to Joseph, and, to Mary and her bulging belly.

"You fool! Why do you debate? Run him and his pregnant mare into the ground, just like the rest!"

"Or," another soldier leered, "run him to the ground, and leave her, for now, to us."

Joseph backed up in the defensive stance he had been taught, many years before, as a boy, his arms spread out, to shield Mary, and at the ready for attack.

The second soldier reached for his belt, and pulled his broadsword, holding it upward.

It was the last thing he ever did.

Whizzing through the air, a four-pronged metal star as large as a man's chest sheared with razor death, tearing through the soldier's neck and sending his head sailing, his body drooping to the ground.

The steel hurricane hurtled unabated, boomeranging back into the hand of the man who had thrown it.

Joseph and Mary gasped as they saw the man who had saved them emerge from the shadows. His body was long and tawny, clad in dark robes and leather ropes tied about him, making him look all the more wraith-like. His hands were sheathed in metal gloves, yet like no metal they had ever seen, almost like liquid, yet ebony, shimmering and brilliant. His hair was a lightning strike, black as midnight and streaked with strange colors exploding from beneath an onyx helmet. The wild locks curled about his haunting face, his silver eyes, haloed in coaled smears, his cheeks ebony knives of flesh, his jaw clenched and strong.

With a click, a visor shield dropped from the helmet down before his face and his visage was fearsome and strange, an endless darkness across which three crimson slashes burst in a macabre death mask.

In each hand he bore an occult, deadly, weapon, a four-pronged short sword, a gleaming claw held in the middle by his bound black-gloved hands around leather-wrapped straps and a large hunk of moonstone embedded in the center, glowing, throbbing.

He cleaved from the dark, stepped in front of Joseph and Mary, between them and the soldiers and called out to the centurions.

"The girl is mine," he said, in a deep, echoing voice. "Let her go immediately."

"The girl is a witch and heretic," one soldier said. "She shall serve us and die as the devil whore she is."

"She shall do neither," the wraith of a man said, striding towards the soldiers.

"Turn and go," another soldier called, "by the order of the Roman Empire!"

"I answer to a higher order," he said, and he blasted towards them, his star-swords whirling and smashing into flesh and bone as the soldiers leapt into battle.

The first centurion was quickly decapitated by a whizzing blade, the second by a steel fang to the gut, another slashed through the neck as he tried to attack from behind, yet another decapitated with one deadly bite of the wraith's furiously spinning blade.

The fifth swung and the darkling barely dodged his steel, the swipe of wind writhing past the fearsome mask, and then the wraith countered with a killing blow through the soldier's chest armor, into his heart.

The last soldier, who had first approached Joseph and Mary, had timidly remained away from the fray, petrified. His eyes were caked with fear from the onset and all the more so upon seeing his brethren cut down so quickly. He fled, but the wraith reached into the pouch around his belt, grabbed a smaller throwing star and whipped it as the man was kicking his horse to escape.

The shuriken was true, but the panicked horse's herky-jerky movements caused the target to warp, and instead of the star lacing through the man's jugular, stopping him cold, it instead lodged in his shoulder, causing him an obvious amount of pain as he screamed, but allowed him to continue on, away, away.

Away as a warning. A message.

One the wraith did not want to see delivered.

He whipped two more shuriken but to no avail, as they wounded but could not deliver a killing blow.

And rapidly into the distance, the soldier and his horse disappeared.

The darkling warrior, undaunted, doffed his helmet and sheathed his star swords. He turned to the little girl, helped her up, covered her in a cloak, and comforted her. She held him tight and thanked him profusely.

"I am sorry I did not reach you sooner," the wraith said. "I had to take care of a few others."

"I am sorry I got separated from you," the girl said, holding him close. "I know you told me to stay by your side. I tried to fight them, but, I do not know what happened."

The man held her tight. "I am just glad you are alright and I got here in time."

The ebon-clad man picked the girl up in his arms, then the two turned to Joseph and Mary, and the warrior nodded to them.

"You had best make your way, and carefully," the wraith said. "Herod's armies are on the purge, killing all the mothers and newborns, for fear of the prophecy of a newborn king, and you are not safe. I wish you Godspeed."

He turned to leave.

"Wait," Joseph called. "We thank you with our life, and yet we do not even know your name."

The wraith turned.

"I am John, of Patmos, of the Vadimikai. Men call me The Revelator."

"I am Joseph, and this is my wife, Mary," Joseph said, waving a hand in front of his wife and, slowly, almost beyond perception, flashing a slight occult signal in his gesture. "We thank you and pray you go with God in your journeys."

The Revelator nodded to them, and then turned to go, striding a step, and then, recognizing the signal, he stopped and turned to them again.

"Joseph," he said. "Of what house?

Joseph smiled. "Of the house of David."

The Revelator's face broke for a moment and he looked at the girl, whose head emerged from his shoulder.

The girl smiled. "Joseph. A kind name for a kind man."

"And this is Mary," Joseph said to the girl, as his wife nodded and smiled.

The Revelator and the girl turned fully to Joseph and Mary and strode to them.

"You know of me," The Revelator said, looking Joseph in the eye. "And I know of you. And you know you must come with us."

Joseph looked at Mary, then at the Revelator, and nodded, as they quickly moved toward the Revelator's home.

"You know we have little time, but must quickly prepare for your journey," the Revelator said.

They hid their horses and entered the dwelling, and then, with a few shifts of stones, found themselves in front of a secret compartment going downward, below the unassuming hovel.

The Revelator nodded to them to follow the steps and Joseph complied, Mary behind him and the Revelator and the girl shadowing their path until they entered a comfortable, secure space teeming with scrolls and esoteric items.

"So beautiful. So beautiful," the girl said, looking at Mary.

"Thank you," Mary said.

"And what is your name?" Joseph said, kindly, to the girl.

The girl looked up to him and smiled.

"I, am Magdalene."

EIGHTEEN

The Arimathean's golden burned parchment eyes darted about the ancient marble room of the Temple of Mars, seizing on an ominous array of figures. Through the incense-heavy fog cloaking the room, he could make out the noose of bodies, clad in tight black, closing around him.

His sword cut an elaborate pattern through the haze, stopping just in front of him in a defensive stance, before slicing lightning-quick to stop the first attacker's thrust.

He leapt above the clashing weapons of two others, his feet landing heavy on the face of a third, blood and spit exploding onto the floor.

The Arimathean hurtled forward, cracking into the soft midsection of an attacking warrior before delivering the full of his sword into another man's chin and swinging his short knife into the neck of a flailing figure at his back.

For a split second a spark of recognition and precognition froze the Arimathean and he leapt again, avoiding a pair of nets that lurched clumsily into one another like drunken brawlers. With a slam of his feet to the ground, the Arimathean captured the strands and yanked his attackers together in a deadly crash of skulls.

Hurtling their bodies around him as a mighty weapon he smashed two more lunging attackers into thick marble pillars and after dropping the limp frames, he flung himself into a corner, pulled a small crystal from his robe and whipped it to the floor.

With a high-pitched shatter the room exploded in violet, incandescent light, the fog balling into drops of water that died to the ground, revealing the five remaining men before him, blinded and grimacing.

Wasting no time, long fingers flashing into his robe, his arm whipped around the room and five razor-sharp shuriken downed the rest in splatters of blood.

But was it the rest?

The Arimathean's eyes furtively scanned the bodies on the floor, counting all he had spied before jumping into the fray. All... but one.

A split second.

There was a slight slit in the air, a rending of the space behind him, as a sword was being raised, a figure sliding around a pillar.

But the Arimathean had already sensed his presence, had already captured the weak will of his prey in his mind's talons.

The Arimathean turned in a blur, his hand outreached, fingers curved in a claw.

Their eyes met.

And the sword, headed for the Arimathean's heart, stopped in mid-air, just before his outstretched hand.

The attacking man's arms and body froze, his face a frightened mask, his teeth gritted in a futile effort to continue his strike to the Arimathean's chest. Sweat dripping down his face, his arm quivered as he struggled to continue his sword's flight, but he stood paralyzed, the sword remaining suspended. His muscles tensed, pulsed, strained, but he could not move.

Holding the man's gaze, the Arimathean's eyes were aglow, turning lighter, lighter, until almost clear, and then, the briefest of sparks flickered in them, and the would-be attacker crumpled like a marionette with its strings cut as his heart exploded in his chest.

Death hung over the room like a morning fog. The Arimathean surveyed the carnage warily, before sensing all was calm, and raised a sleeve to wipe his brow.

Across the room a sliver of light widened as a door opened and a man in long, white robes appeared. He opened his spindly, ivory paw to reveal a black stone, covered in white runes and one, huge, magnificent ruby. He lifted it to shatter it upon the ground, but in one clean move, the Arimathean whipped a knife across the room, impaling the man's arm against the wall, the charm still clutched in it, now immovable, then threw another knife, impaling the man's second hand, disabling it as well.

The wizard in white tried psychic attack, tried enchantment, but to no avail. His attacker was Arimathean, was of the Glowing City, his mind was impenetrable to a human mage.

The Arimathean crossed the room to the enchanter, grabbed the charm out of his hand and ripped his arm from the wall with a violent thrust. The wizard screamed and cried, and the Arimathean whipped the robed man's arm behind him and clenched a muscular arm around the wizard's neck.

"Your silence will buy you nothing but death," the Arimathean snapped.

"If I speak to you, my death is slow by Herod," the man whined.

"What is to make you think it will not be slower and more sinister by me?"

With a subtle twist of his hand the Arimathean jerked the man's arm slightly, causing him to wail in pain.

"Speak the truth or speak no more! And watch in agony as the animals fight to feast upon your tongue, ripped fresh from your lying mouth, while I decide how to destroy the rest of you."

"I know not who you seek," the robed man sputtered.

The Arimathean dug his fingers into the wizard's neck, drawing blood and sending a bolt of pain through the man's body.

"You know damn well who I am looking for," the Arimathean growled. "Either I rip the words from your throat or you surrender them willingly. Your choice."

NINETEEN

Ornate high-backed chairs stood in orderly rows against the inner sanctum of Herod's throne room. In each of them, a man of some stature within the kingdom eagerly awaited the night's festivities and feast.

Herod's throne had been placed at the head of the titanic space, now bereft of the pretense of the curtains, now dominated by the pit of fire and the deadly spears jutting from it. The king sat atop his bejeweled perch, grinning demonically and issuing orders to scurrying servants, who genuflected and capitulated rapidly, petrified of becoming part of the menu.

The chief seer, Ozmondias, hovered alongside his king, periodically making note of some barely perceptible detail and whispering in Herod's ear, invariably causing the king to smirk, glower or raise an eyebrow impishly.

Behind them was an awful, twisted mess of thorny branches dripping blood, a demented crown of spikes, wrapped around a huge oval mirror that, rather than reflecting the room, simmered with an opaque mist. And on either side of the mirror were three of The Six.

The high priests continued to drip their perverse spells while circling the room, the monks' chants droned on as they stood unmoving at each corner.

Before the pit was a sad, broken jigsaw of a naked, sweaty mess of slaves, whipped bloody and compliant, being kept in line by a huge wall of centurions on either side.

Behind them, in chains, were the Magi.

As the three, still fully wrapped in the fine clothing of mystics and lords, were pushed into the room at the point of several spears, the crowd of nobles began to buzz and gasp. Herod laughed and clapped his hands mockingly.

"As you see, we have some delectable additions to the menu," he said, before clapping his hands loudly to silence the room. "I think you will find them quite rich."

Herod and the nobles laughed, but the reverie was broken by a messenger rushing into the room, bowing to Herod before being summoned to his throne. The messenger handed Herod a scroll and whispered to Herod and Ozmondias, who conferred. Then, as Herod dispatched the messenger, Ozmondias turned to The Six, spoke animatedly to them and handed the scroll to one of them, who nodded, and then led the gigantic, fearsome warriors from the room.

The Magi, noticing all of this, looked to one another.

Herod glanced at Ozmondias and smiled, pulling the seer closer to him, speaking sotto voce, before turning again to those assembled.

"Again, it is my pleasure for you to once more feast with the one, true and only," Herod looked deviously at the Magi, "king of the Empire."

The arrayed nobles cheered and laughed, saluting the throne, and Herod lapped up their obsequious gesture.

Addressing the Magi, he said, "As you are also men of royal blood, I will grant you the opportunity to beg me for your lives."

"And as you are also a man of royal blood, we shall extend the same courtesy," Balthazar said.

Herod smiled.

"Balthazar, I think I will enjoy devouring you most of all."

Herod turned to the hooded men on either side of the pits, and the soldiers around the slaves.

"Prepare the fires and march them in on my command!"

The hooded men took long, steel spears and began raking the flames higher and higher, until they lashed and sizzled over the spikes of the pit and caused a slow steam to rise through the room. The smell of crackled, old, burned flesh from the pit's previous victims began to fill the space, and Herod breathed in deeply with relish.

But along with it, grew a curious smoke.

It started a barely perceptible white whisp but soon turned gray and thick.

The nobles thought little of it, as did Herod and the others, until it began to blossom and weave about all, causing Herod and Ozmondias to turn to one another in puzzlement and then, a rapid lucidity and a mixture of anger and fear.

Too late, Herod realized, what was happening, and he called out desperately.

"Guards! Into the pit with them! All of them!"

But the order was useless as the cloud completely blanketed the room, making it impossible to see more than a few inches to either side.

"Guards!" shouted Herod. "The gates! The door!"

The clatter of armor and the tumult of scrambling to find the levers to drop the gates clanged through the impenetrable mist, along with the shuffle of countless bodies moving, running to escape.

"Ozmondias!"

Ozmondias was already chanting in a deep, guttural voice, struggling to part the mists, to disperse them, but the wind he summoned was anemic and faint compared to the fevered charms of the Magi and the fog remained stubborn and turgid.

When the gate finally dropped, silence filled the room, as thick and ominous as the vapors, and then, the cries of death slammed off its walls, along with the echoes of armor falling to the hard ground or into the deadly maw of the fire pit.

However, as the battle raged, the mists dissipated, the Magi no longer able to fully maintain their spell and their concentration on the battle at hand. Before long, the vapors had risen to reveal the naked servants all having fled, leaving the three Magi, weapons drawn, chains dissipated to ash, alone among a plague of dead centurions, more than a dozen of which were impaled upon the feasting spits.

However, the corpses did not mark all those at Herod's disposal.

Warily, the remaining soldiers, who still outnumbered the Magi four to one, circled the three men.

But then, suddenly, the odds became less daunting, as five centurions were quickly felled by whirring shuriken blades thrown from above. Into the mess of confused soldiers, the Arimathean landed heavily, screaming a blood-curdling battle cry, massive swords in both mighty fists, sending blood and flesh and heads forever emblazoned with stunned expressions flying about the room in a shower of crimson doom.

The Magi rapidly took advantage of the chaos to dispatch the rest of the troops with hurtling shuriken and whirling blades, and then, as Herod's servants rang the bells for more men to replace them, Balthazar turned and with a wave of his hand sent forth a massive wall of white-hot flame, melting the gates before them. As he did, Melchior lifted both arms and once more the room began to fill with a heavy fog as dozens of soldiers stampeded into the murky air.

"Fools!" Herod cried. "Rush them! It is only smoke! It is only an illusion!"

But then the mist ran caliginous, morphing, and a vile buzz pocked the room as the clouds transformed into a feverish army of wasps that coated the soldiers, whose cries spiked as they flailed in confusion.

Ozmondias, his fish-belly countenance dripping with sweat in concentration, conjured up a roaring dragon beast of burnt orange and darkened brown flame that engulfed the swarm and turned it to coal dust, but not before the soldiers were spent and the Magi and the Arimathean were long gone.

Gone in frantic pursuit of The Six.

TWENTY

They traveled by horseback, through the desert, avoiding the hearts of towns as much as possible to escape any potential detection. Joseph and the Revelator knew that the surviving soldier had to have made his way back to Herod by now, and that the Romans would know where they had been and possibly what path they were taking. Herod's eyes would be everywhere. Their only hope was to outwit them and to hope that Herod did not know where they were ultimately headed.

The Revelator looked to the skies as they traveled, seeking telltale signs – birds or animals or tricks of the elements that seemed out of the ordinary -- that would herald the subtle rift of their world about its seams and betray the presence of demonic forces.

Up until now, Herod had deployed soldiers in his quest to kill the infant and his parents. But soldiers were slow and human and could be defeated by those skilled in the deadly crafts, even if those soldiers were protected by charms. Before long, the Revelator knew, Herod would eschew his centurions completely, and turn to otherworldly means.

Or, he feared all the more, Herod would have help in obtaining them.

As much as Herod feared a new king, Satan would fear him all the more, and if the former were to overcome his own trepidation over use of the deepest of Luciferian arts and the latter were to somehow find a way to manifest in this world, or summon forth his sinister flock, the Revelator and his companions would find themselves facing far more formidable foes than those of sinew and steel.

The Revelator meditated upon this, seeking a solution, but found little more than resolve and faith to guide him.

He looked ahead to the couple.

Joseph rode alongside Mary, doting on her, watching over her. They would stop periodically to rest, to give her water and food, and he would hold her in his arms and look into her eyes, kiss her tenderly, kiss her bulging belly and talk to the child inside. More often than not, he would give her his portion of food and water, and would only imbibe when she insisted upon it.

"They love each other very much," Magdalene said to the Revelator, from a distance, as they gathered strength and nourishment.

"Yes, they do," he said. "If only the people of the world loved each other as that of a good husband and wife, parents and child."

"Why does Herod want them killed?" the girl asked. "If the baby is truly the one prophesized then why would he not want peace?"

"Herod is a man of power, and therefore he is a man of fear, to keep the masses in line and retain his throne," the Revelator said. "He fears losing what he holds, and when a man lives by war, he fears being made useless by peace."

After another brief distance had been covered, Joseph called to his companions, and they stopped, so Mary could rest. Joseph disembarked from his horse and pulled water from a pack, handing it to Mary, then he caressed her arm reassuringly and spoke softly to her.

The Revelator and Magdalene remained apart from them, scanning the area for any potential threats. The girl watched Mary and Joseph, smiling and laughing, in stark contrast to their dour guardians.

"How can they be so happy when things are so grim?" the girl asked.

"It is precisely when they are so grim that it is most important to be so happy," the Revelator said.

"But still," Magdalene said, "I sense within him an unease, as if he is fully aware of the perils that lie before us, yet he maintains the façade to lighten her bearing, to maintain her spirit."

"He knows the road ahead," the ebon-clad man said. "It is no accident he is with her. No accident they are who they are. It was destined. As it was destined for us to be with them now, for as long as we may be."

The girl looked at him and saw his face run turbulent as he scanned the sky. A lightning flash appeared strangely in the distance. Materializing from it, seeping out, came a splash of black, creeping fingers through the firmament, that coagulated into an array of murky figures, sailing high, over the place they had left behind.

"We had best be moving on to the next town, to find safe haven," the Revelator said, rising up and motioning to Joseph to likewise begin the trek again.

The girl looked up at her mentor but his eyes did not meet hers. They only remained on the horizon, fixed, as a scowl tightened on his face.

TWENTY-ONE

They could see the town off just a way, so close, the light of fresh torches beckoning as the skies began to dusk, and each of them, weary, seemed to sag a bit in the saddle, breathing a heavy sigh.

Still in the distance, hard against the setting sun, fading into the night, the ominous figures soared and circled, but remained afar from the four pilgrims.

Joseph turned to wave to the Revelator and Magdalene. The man nodded to Joseph and they stopped for a moment, as Joseph reached into a saddlebag to give his wife a cool drink and gingerly wipe her head with a soft cloth. The Revelator and Magdalene pulled up alongside them.

"I am sorry, but we must stop again," Joseph said, easing off his horse to care for Mary. "My wife has become extremely tired, unusually so, and is not feeling well."

The Revelator nodded, and he and Magdalene circled them slowly. The hair on the back of his neck had stiffened and his guts churned. He did not know why, but he did not like it, and he felt the sudden need to be much closer to them.

"I understand," the Revelator said. "I have felt the same weight. I do not know wherefrom it emerges, but . . ."

It was then he noticed it.

The sound of the wings.

The dark figures, now swirling overhead.

Birds.

Ravens.

Cackling.

It started low at first, weak and faint, barely perceptible, and then, just slightly, their garments began to quiver, and they felt the cold wind blowing in, ever stronger, behind them.

Mary shivered, and Joseph pulled his own cloak from his back to shield around her.

"We have to go, now," the Revelator said. "We need to get to the city."

The Revelator watched as Joseph leapt upon his horse again and he and Mary started moving towards the lights of the town.

He and Magdalene matched them, riding right behind.

The Revelator looked down at the girl.

"Magdalene, you know what to do."

She nodded and quickly dipped into a small pouch astride her horse, pulling out two delicate rune stones and a handful of sparkling, pungent dust. She grasped the stones in a fist as she swung her arm around her horse, steadying herself, and threw the dust into the air with the other hand. Instead of quickly dissipating into the stream behind them, the glittering particles hovered and clung about them, spreading around the riders as Magdalene and the Revelator uttered a prayer, three times without ending, then pausing, then three times again, then pausing, then three times once more, as they spurred their horses forward to get as close to Mary and Joseph as they could.

They felt the cold wind begin to blow, harder and more forcefully, and on it they heard a high, pitched, screeching cackle, and with it a low, diabolical voice, uttering at first words they could only strain to hear, but then whispering the most foul and depraved scenes of debauchery into their ears.

The Revelator grasped an amulet around his neck, looked to Magdalene as she held the jewels in her hand, and the winds went silent. She grabbed another handful of glimmering dust from the pouch and threw it into the air. They uttered the prayers, once, twice, three times.

They spurred their horses forward feverishly as a faint silver outline began to form around them, around Joseph and

Mary. The shield enveloped them and shadowed them, enclosing them as they descended over the hill and into the city.

Behind them, they could see, as the night encroached, the blazing eyes, the flames of the nostrils, of The Six and their horses, huge, burned-skin steeds, spewing steam and tar behind them as they pounded the sand and rock. Above, the birds were circling, circling, tighter and tighter, their sardonic calls alerting the demons to the presence of the fleeing prey. The demons whipped closer, closer, while the birds waited, waited, for their sup, the dead flesh of the recently slain, to pluck fresh and call their own.

Dread closed around them like a fist. The four were almost to the city when The Revelator glanced over his shoulder just in time to see the largest of The Six smash his weapon into their mystical shield.

Then another.

And another.

It held fast, until, three demons in unison crushed their weapons into it, and in a hail of sparks, a small crack formed.

Casting his steely gaze backward, the Revelator conjured a force field knocking the demons away for a moment, buying the four fleeing a few seconds of time.

But it wasn't enough.

Like sharks upon wounded prey, The Six closed around them and began raining down unearthly fire upon the shield the Revelator and Magdalene had conjured, charring and battering it and finally smashing a huge hole in it, the force wave and repercussion battering the Revelator and Magdalene and forcing them off their steeds and smashing them onto the hard ground, tumbling down, away, as the demons frenzied down on them.

Joseph looked back as the shield about Joseph and Mary likewise disintegrated in a chaotic shower of sparks, causing their horses to ease up in fear.

The Revelator glared at them.

"You must get to the city!"

The man and woman looked at each other, still stunned, then looked back at the two protecting them.

Tears budded in Mary's eyes as she watched the demons froth and flail, their shapes horribly distorting in blood-colored messes as their earthly forms were disrupted attempting to smash and destroy a second holy shield the Revelator had quickly thrown up around him, Magdalene, Mary and Joseph.

The little girl looked to the man and woman.

"You must . . .!"

"But we cannot leave you!" Mary said.

"Go, now!" the Revelator called to Joseph. "We won't be able to hold them much . . ."

At that moment, the new shield collapsed in a white light that turned the night to day for a second, blinding The Six and sending them scrambling and screeching, their dark steeds hurtling and throwing them as they buckled.

Stunning them, keeping them at bay.

But only for a moment.

The shields were gone, now only a glittering mist keeping the skies illumined as they hovered, and slowly drifted to the ground about them, allowing neither hunters nor prey access to the stealth of the growing darkness. Amidst the dreamily turgid dust enveloping and lighting the air, the demons regrouped, grabbed their weapons and struck at the two, as the Revelator's star-blades whirred into his hands and Magdalene's black-runed sai into hers.

The first of The Six zealously threw himself in full at the Revelator, cackling horribly as his long sword slashed the shrieking air, biting at the man. He dodged and parried, while advancing closer and closer to the demon, until finally with blinding speed he whirled, slicing shallowly into the demon's chest with one blade while whipping another star-sword back around to dismember one of the demons' hands at the wrist, the darkling's weapon falling to the ground.

With a kick, the Revelator sent the wounded, but still live, body into three of the others, and glanced to Magdalene, trying valiantly to fend off another two. The pair of warriors, man and girl, were the only shield now between the demons and the couple.

Joseph and Mary.

Frozen, indecisive, unsure whether to remain, in peril but also within protection, or try to flee, and hope the demons wouldn't follow.

The Revelator whirled to Magdalene, in battle, quickly pulled a holy knife from his belt and whipped it into the right eye of the demon fighting her, causing it to emit a blood-chilling shriek and jerk back, buying her time.

He turned again to Mary and Joseph, conflicted as they watched the two fighting, not wanting to turn their backs as they potentially met their doom.

"We will hold them off as long as we can! Worry not about our fates, we have pledged to protect your own!"

The Revelator heard a hoarse growl beside him, smelled the acrid tint in the air and moved just in time to avoid an axe from one of The Six and a spiked mace from another. He hurtled sideways, the moonstones of his star-blades glowing bright and hurtling plasma bolts at the two, wounding them, but unfortunately only wounding, buying time.

Behind him another demon savaged at him, the darkling metal scything the halo of drifting dust encircling them. He felt the singe of steel slice through the armor of his shoulder and the sting of blood down his arm, but, aided by his sacred precognition and superhuman reflexes, had moved quickly enough to avoid doom.

While the hell spawn were off balance he buried his star blade in one, shoving it deep into its gullet, the sacred stone at the center of the blade drilling into its heart, causing the demon to quake and scream and explode, finally dying, finally killing one of The Six, as another leapt toward the Revelator, who moved just in time to avoid it and sent it tumbling.

He looked again to Magdalene as she was being pushed, pushed, back further and further away from him by the dual demon attacks. Their jaws clamped sickly, drool dripping from them raining down on her as their swords smashed down on hers. Her sai swirled in valiant attempts to parry the demon blades, as she uttered prayers to gain her strength, the protective amulet around her neck a beacon, burning in the night with holy power to keep her sustained, to keep her alive.

Until with one blow, barely blocked by her crossed sai, a demon sent her tumbling down, away from its death blow, but still, horribly weakening her.

The Revelator hurled his star-blades around him, slamming them into the earth, and a cloud of sand and dust whipped up. He sent it cascading towards the demons attacking

Magdalene, creating a temporary force shield. Then with another whip of his arm into the earth, the moonstone of his blades burning bright, he sent another shield circling around him, briefly blinding the demons about to pounce upon him and shoving them back hard to the earth. He looked back to Joseph and Mary, still frozen in uncertainty.

"We have to go, Mary, we must," Joseph said.

She remained still, her steed unmoving.

"But we cannot just let them die, we…"

"We have to have faith, in them, in God, and in our path ahead," Joseph said. "We must go."

The Revelator looked to Magdalene, the demons now circling her hungrily. He cast force shields at them, knocking one back hard, sailing into the distance, but the other, which had spun away, was only glanced aside.

The demon, merely stunned, lunged at Magdalene as the girl futilely raised her arms and sai in a pathetic attempt to fend off the attack. Weakened, she could only offer a quick prayer as the demon's sword was raised and rained down upon her, an earthquake upon her blades, slamming her back to the ground.

The Revelator tried to throw a spell to protect her, but couldn't complete it, dodging two demon strikes leveled at him.

The Revelator glanced at Mary and Joseph.

Joseph looked to Mary, then back to the Revelator and Magdalene, and then he realized what he needed to do. To protect his wife and unborn son. And he spurred his horse forward, and hers as well, as they fled towards the city.

But they had waited too long.

One of the demons had circled around the Revelator and Magdalene, and was now blocking the way to their escape, drooling and cackling as its horse leapt towards them, knocking the man and woman off their steeds and to the ground.

"Mary!" Joseph cried, recovering and leaping to his pregnant wife's side.

But just as he arrived, the demon was there, sword raised, ready to destroy them.

TWENTY-TWO

The demon's weapon slashed viciously downward at the woman, its steel lusting for her exposed, ivory neck. Instead, it was flung backwards and smashed into the earth, embedded and stuck, as a gust of wind shoved the hades-spawn back, tumbling to the dirt.

The demon's last act was to look in the direction of the mystic attack, only to see Gaspar's hurled axe explode into its face, knocking it lifeless to the ground.

The remaining four demons turned from their prey, and the Magi and the Arimathean were upon them, swords drawn, teeth gritted, slashing and stabbing at them ferociously. They, and the Revelator, pushed the hell-spawn back, away from Joseph, Mary and the weakened, wounded Magdalene.

The demons split the sky with squeals and spells. The birds, under the hellions' command, shrilled and jerked. Their eyes going red, their claws bared, they hurtled downward at the holy warriors, diving at them, ripping at their flesh, distracting them as the four living of The Six continued to attack.

Balthazar spun back from the fray, threw his cloak about him in a typhoon of sparks and chanted an ancient prayer, thrusting his arms skyward, raining sacred ash to the heavens as it turned to flame, snaking around in a silver-blue streak as it decimated the avian attack.

No longer battling from the skies as well, Melchior's slithering blade was concentrated solely on its demon prey, blocking one monster's sword before slicing through its defenses and across its neck to halt it. And then, with a quicksilver thrust, the Magi pounded the blade down into the demon's heart to send it back to hell.

The Revelator, star blades spinning feverishly to halt killing blows from another demon's jagged weapons, tumbled aside as the demon's ebon bladed attack slammed earthward. He spun rapidly to slice out the beast's legs, throwing it on its chest, and then, with a dual explosion through its back his blades decimated the demon's armor and penetrated its oozing boil of a heart, splitting it open in a fit of slime and sulphur.

Gaspar and the demon before him had crashed their swords into one another with such fury that both saw their steel sail to the ground. They sprung at one another, battling hand-to-hand. Gaspar had been thrown onto his back, felt the demon's icy grasp around him as its distended fangs reached down to his face, its serpentine tongue extending, looking to feast upon the Magi's dark features.

But Gaspar's herculean paw crushed the demon's proboscis in its grasp and with a titanic jab, the Magi sent his forehead smashing into the demon's orbital bone. The explosive attack stunned the demon for a moment, and then with a powerful grasp, the man closed his huge hands around the demon's neck, uttering a prayer of exorcism, sacred and ancient, to weaken it and then crushing its spine in two decimating, disgusting jerks of his fists.

The Arimathean, two heavy swords exploding against the demon blades before him, their muscles flaring with each ear-splitting smash of steel in attack, got inside the demon's reach and thrust its arms aside, exposing its heart. With a feral attack of both glimmering fangs, he impaled the beast, the blades knuckles deep into its chest, as he let out a mighty cry and ripped upwards, tearing the demon's torso apart.

Spent, wounded and doused in sweat, blood and demon bile, the warriors rose to look at each other and to the woman, man and child they fought to protect, as in the distance, soaring from the carnage, a lone raven cawed.

Joseph held Mary, comforting her as she clasped one arm around him and another snugly circling her belly.

The Arimathean glanced across the battleground. "Where is the girl?"

Magdalene.

She was nowhere near them.

They quickly scanned the ground but found nothing in their immediate vicinity.

Balthazar reached into his pouch and produced a tiny, translucent pebble, which he rubbed quickly and threw to the earth, shattering it with a burst of light. As it smoldered and sparked, a low fog of illumination began to blanket the earth, spreading out from them, seeping past the blood and sand and decrepit oozing tar remains of the demons' bodies, until it found a slight bolt of ghost white, a tiny arm, motionless behind a rock.

The Revelator leapt to the body to find the girl, still and bleeding.

He put her mouth to his cheek.

Put her heart to his ear.

"She is still there," he said, "barely."

The Magi descended upon her, Balthazar and Melchior attending to her, praying over her, applying salves to her wounds.

Her breathing eked forth, intermittently, strained and stained with blood and fluid.

Her heart thumped slowly, feebly.

"We have to get her to the city," the Revelator said. "She has no chance, without…"

"No," Balthazar said, holding one long-fingered hand out to him, "she has every chance."

Melchior kneeled over the girl, placing his hands over her head.

"She has every chance," Balthazar said.

He glanced back at the couple, as Mary's hand went to her belly. Joseph looked down at her, concerned, putting his arm around her.

"What is wrong?" he said.

"The baby," she said.

"Is he?"

"He's, I feel, he's fine, he's just, I just…"

Melchior closed his eyes, his hands now both on the girl's head, as he felt an energy rush through him, and into her. He felt the skies collide and open up, felt as if the two of them were engulfed in a beam of light, lilting down from the heavens, through him, through her.

It lasted for just a moment, but it was enough.

The girl's eyes flickered. She coughed. And then, gingerly, she put her hands to her chest, and opened her eyes, looking at the retreating light in the sky above her, then at the concerned faces of those around her.

"I... I ... is everything alright?" she sputtered weakly.

"All is well, my child," Balthazar said with a warm, reassuring grin. "All is well."

He looked up, and his eyes met Mary's, her hands still upon her belly, slowly circling the infant moving inside, who was calming, calming once more.

TWENTY-THREE

Entering the small town under the cover of night, following the secret symbols few but they knew how to decipher, the group found safe haven in the caverns beneath a shopkeeper's storefront.

The paranoia of the Roman Empire and its proxies, particularly under Herod, and its subsequent suppression and tyranny, had only made the clandestine societies all the more prevalent and clever, and had likewise caused them to expand their networks. Within almost every settlement was at least one man, ostensibly a merchant, carpenter or cleric, whose store featured a world below it, secret chambers that may go forever unused, but were there in case they were needed.

Some housed rare, ancient scrolls. Others harbored sacred artifacts or holy objects with mystical properties. And yet a few more, rarer still, acted as hubs for preparation, for just a moment such as this, when the stars had aligned as the seers had said they would, and a child, unlike others, would be born, as the prophets had decreed.

Cages of doves were among the signs of potential hospitality in such a situation. The birds were bred and kept among the storekeepers, tiny avatars of white and black and red. They traveled to and from the ancient cities, between those in the secret societies, to those along strategic byways to keep them wary of the possibility of their service being needed along the way.

Among those in receipt of such an elegant prize was the man who owned the shop the fugitives found themselves seeking refuge in as they slumped into the town, weary from battle. His name was Zechariah, and he lived with his wife Ezra, their youngest son, Matthew, and their eldest daughter, Bellaropa, who had only recently returned from exile, from captivity, with her likewise captive husband, Benjamin.

Benjamin and Bellaropa had previously known a life as shepherds, a life to which they yearned to return, but could not yet do so. They remained under the roof of her father, tending to wounds they had suffered while they were slaves, captives to the wicked king Herod.

Captives, tortured and terrified, on the cusp of death, who had been set free, only at the last possible moment, just recently.

Set free, by three men they happened to see shadow the front door of Bellaropa's father's shop.

Not wanting to betray the horror they had experienced and bring dishonor to their house, they had remained silent, and the Magi likewise, but in a private moment, Benjamin and Bellaropa gave thanks to the men who had saved them, gratitude they had neither the time nor the opportunity to give in their zeal to flee Herod's palace.

In addition to their verbal appreciation, they presented the Magi with a gift, a small ivory horn, and instructions on its import.

The Magi bowed in gratitude, thanking them copiously for their offering, and pledging their silence in regard to the more sordid details of their previous meeting.

And in exchange, Benjamin and Bellaropa, and their family, provided the fugitives with comfortable shelter, rooms which would serve for rest, however brief, on this rigorous journey.

It was in one of these rooms that Joseph and Mary were stationed, in as much comfort as could be provided, with Magdalene likewise tended to.

When they got to their room, Joseph could tell Mary was spent, and he lifted her into his arms and carried her to the bed. He laid her down, but she would not let him go. She grabbed onto him tight, tighter, tighter, until the growing sobs and flood of tears from her eyes erupted forth in his embrace.

"I know," Joseph said. "I know."

She calmed, tears still streaming, and pulled away slightly, looking into his eyes.

"I knew, I had been told, I had, the visions had, but, I, I had no idea, I did not know," Mary said, awash in tears.

She held him tight again.

"I remember the purges, our father and mother hiding us, the children of the towns being secreted away, but some, some missing and never seen when we finally emerged," Mary said. "But they always seemed so far away. Stories. Tales told to warn, to keep us wary. But even the purges were not the same as this. Not the same as, as, being hunted."

"But we are not alone, we must have faith, God has sent us men of great power to protect us on our journey," Joseph said.

Mary caught her breath and began to calm.

"You are right, He has protected us," she said, looking at Joseph.

Joseph nodded.

"We must have faith," she said.

She lay down and Joseph placed his hand on her face, caressing her cheek, and she was fast asleep.

He kissed her forehead, watched over her a moment, then padded softly from the room, approaching the Magi, the Revelator and the Arimathean.

"I know why you have come, and why you follow and protect us," Joseph said. "We have experienced the same visions, been shown the same prophecy. But while some commitment can be called a duty to human decency, such vociferous and passionate a defense as you offer is only contingent upon faith at best. So, we thank you."

"We are at your service," Balthazar said, nodding.

"I understand," Joseph said. "You know I was once of your order, and I know the devotion involved."

"Indeed, we know well of your past," Melchior said.

"Nevertheless, I want you to know how deeply we appreciate your help," Joseph said.

He looked to the room where Mary rested.

"I cannot imagine my life without her," Joseph said, sighing. "Without them."

He looked down, then up at the Magi again.

"Thank you," Joseph said. "You cannot know how much it means to me."

The Arimathean paused for a moment, silent, then looked at Joseph.

"We do."

They exchanged glances, and Joseph gave them a slight smile, then adjourned to lay down with his wife.

Melchior, Gaspar and the Revelator slept downstairs with the three most vulnerable while Balthazar and the Arimathean took their turn as sentinels upstairs, sitting at a table, the Arimathean downing the last of an old bottle.

"I know what you are thinking Balthazar," the Arimathean said.

Balthazar laughed. "And I thought I was the oracle here, my friend."

"I do not need to be a seer to see right through you," the Arimathean growled, taking a deep drink.

"As always, only you can determine the depth of your doubt," Balthazar said.

"It was coincidence, nothing more," the Arimathean said. "Coincidence about us showing up just in time. About us coming to be at the home of the two freed. About, well, everything to which you might ascribe otherwise."

"As you wish."

"We live in a small world, and you and I both know of the clandestine hand, the shadow societies to which we both belong, and their connections which have brought us here," the Arimathean said, taking a swig. "There is nothing supernatural about it, merely the utilization of a network and coincidence, pure coincidence."

"You seem to wish to convince yourself more than any other," Balthazar said.

"God helps no one," the Arimathean said. "Even if He exists. He helps no one."

"Is that so?"

"Yes."

"And what of the girl?"

"You and Melchior healed that girl with the help of the earth, with herbs and incantations. You are skilled and trained well, but it was nothing more than words, utilizing vibrations in line with magnetic fields to help clear her aura, holistic knowledge passed down from the ancients, through the invisible clans. It had nothing to do with faith or any miracles."

The Arimathean slugged his bottle down firmly.

"Or anyone else."

"Maybe not," Balthazar said. "But maybe."

"Maybe not," the Arimathean said.

"But maybe," Balthazar said, "those abilities, those words, those healing rituals, are gifts in and of themselves, miracles abundant in our world, aside from all else. Gifts from the one true God who permeates and empowers this world."

"And maybe she is just lucky we were there," the Arimathean said. "Or not so lucky she got dragged into this."

"Maybe it was destined to be that we were there, in time?" Balthazar said.

The Arimathean took a huge gulp of the spirit from the dusty vessel and choked it down, gritting his teeth, his forehead furrowed.

"We would not have saved them otherwise," Balthazar said.

"He is awfully choosy about who he decides to save," the Arimathean grumbled.

The men sat in silence.

"The evil men do is from their hearts, not God's," Balthazar said.

"And where do men's hearts come from?"

"Once born, men decide their own paths in this world," Balthazar said. "Whether God's or Satan's or their own."

"Satan," the Arimathean said. "I have seen enough evil in the hearts of men to wonder why you and your mystics and priests even bother with that myth. You have enough evil in this world to scare people without it."

"But the demons you have seen convince you not at all?"

"They are no different than any other beasts that roam the parallel worlds. Just that some are deadlier than the others. They kill. And can be killed."

He looked hard at Balthazar.

"And so can we."

The two men looked out into the night, the candle between them flickering.

"So why do you aid us?" Balthazar said. "Why not devote your time to your quest, to find and kill Herodius? Why did you save us?"

"I have my own reasons."

"I am a mystic, not a psychic."

"That hasn't stopped you from reading minds before."

"I could not read yours if I wanted to. You are Arimathean. And, once, of the Glowing City, of the same order as we three. Your mind is closed to me unless you invite me in."

The Arimathean smirked.

"I know Herodius will not be alone. Gaspar said as much, and as much as I loathe to admit it, I have to agree with him. I might need help to get to him. I figure if I help you, you will help me."

"So, revenge, then."

"Do I need any more reason?" the Arimathean sighed.

"Revenge, my friend, is a dangerous motive," Balthazar said. "Craving revenge is like devouring poison for years and hoping for your foe to die from it."

"Or," the Arimathean said, "like hoarding poison to eventually shove down their throats."

Balthazar steepled his hands and gazed into the darkness, then back at his friend.

"And that is your only reason? Your only drive to help the father, mother and child? And what if you die on this quest and never fulfill your thirst for vengeance?"

The Arimathean grimaced, then, ever slightly, his face lightened.

"Everyone dies," he said. "If there is any honor in this world, any glory, it is in giving your life to someone who deserves it."

His face clenched again.

"And maybe, someone who deserves your life more than you do."

He lifted the bottle to his mouth and drank down the last of it, placed the empty vessel on the table forcefully, and wiped his mouth.

"Like I said, God helps no one," the Arimathean said, rising from the table.

He walked towards the door, looking towards the portal to the family, to the girl, and then back at Balthazar.

"But I do."

TWENTY-FOUR

The men awoke at dawn the next day, to discover the Revelator had yet to sleep, having tended to his young charge all night. He had been her only family since saving her as an infant from an earlier purge and had raised her like a daughter, bringing her up in the ancient arts, out of tradition but also out of protection, should he be killed. At least then, he thought, she might be able to defend herself and make her way in the world.

As Balthazar and the Arimathean padded down the stairs, the Revelator silently greeted them. He looked at the sleeping Magdalene, broken but steadily recovering. He gently stroked her hair aside and kissed her forehead, tucked her blanket around her cozily and walked from the room with the men, meeting Gaspar and Melchior.

They walked up the stairs to where their hosts had prepared breakfast for them. The warriors thanked them for their hospitality, gathered their meals and adjourned to a room apart from the family, to discuss the journey ahead.

"I know you cannot stay, but I cannot go with you, I am all she has, and she cannot continue," the Revelator said.

Balthazar nodded and offered a resigned smile.

"We thank you, my friend, you and your brave young apprentice, for all your help," he said.

"And you know where you must go?" the Revelator said.

Balthazar looked into the main room of the home, where their hosts sat talking with Joseph and Mary, enjoying the meal and the first notes of the day. He watched as they laughed and smiled, exchanged stories, and Joseph lovingly doted on his wife, and she, in return, held him close.

"Yes," Balthazar said.

"And where is that?" the Arimathean said.

"Bethlehem," the Revelator said.

"Bethlehem?" the Arimathean said, surprised. "Why not a larger city where they could disappear among the many?"

Balthazar looked at him.

"It has been foretold."

The Revelator nodded.

"And so it has been foretold, in the hidden book of Micah, that the one they will call messiah would be born in the tiny town of Bethlehem," the Revelator said.

The Arimathean rolled his eyes. "Wherever offers them the best chance to escape this insanity is fine by me."

Bethlehem.

It seemed random and dubious, strange and unsure, to most who had read of its destiny. But not to all, and particularly not to those within the silent hand, the invisible sect that had set aside so many of the sacred texts through the centuries.

Bethlehem.

Foretold.

But hardly arbitrary.

Particularly for those who hewed to the ancient traditions.

Bethlehem was a sacred spire. It sat upon a holy vortex of ley lines – energy beams that cut through and across the earth, magnetic throughways unseen and mostly unheard of, but that nevertheless could have a profound effect, particularly if utilized by those who had been trained in the craft of manipulating and channeling their power.

Those such as the Magi.

In Bethlehem, the stars aligned for precious moments, above and around the city, creating a battlement, a holy pathway, an unimpeachable halo, in which the child could be born and no evil could besmirch him. For only a time, only a short, vital time, but for a time nonetheless.

The heavens had allowed a path, a sacred shield, that could be used to protect the child and his parents. And even in the days beyond it as it dissipated, its resonance could be utilized to fog and confuse evil and allow them to escape, allow them precious time in which to flee beyond its safety while the heavens sought to obfuscate and perturb.

But it was a fortunate circumstance that would only last a set time.

And that time would be nigh.

"We should retreat to the road again," Melchior said. "A storm builds, the skies grow with clouds of sinister shapes, marionettes of a dire theater, and we know Herod's defeats will be short as he attempts to destroy us."

Gaspar nodded towards Joseph and Mary and lowered his voice.

"And it seems her time is near, very near, and she continues to grow weary and weak," he said. "We may not make it before long."

"Then it is good that Bethlehem is not far from here," Melchior said.

The Revelator glanced at Joseph and Mary, then to the Arimathean and the three Magi, motioning them downstairs.

Balthazar caught Zechariah's eye, and in the man's head he heard the voice of the Magi, steeling him to be wary, on guard. The man nodded to Balthazar, and the four warriors were led by the Revelator beyond the secret portal and downstairs, to a shelf of relics, herbs and mystical dusts.

"I have spent the night tending to my young apprentice, but in the moments while she slept, I looked upon the icons here," the Revelator said. "The paths leading to many worlds are open through these shelves. I can help guide you, and if God is with us, you could be to Bethlehem in haste."

They strode to the shelf and began looking about its contents, picking up items of particular note.

Balthazar's long fingers stroked his beard. "These could be utilized for a good many things."

"Including," Melchior said, raising an eyebrow as he looked upon the materials, "a mystical portal."

"Exactly," the Revelator said.

"Haste may tempt, but we must beware," Melchior said. "A door opens more than one way."

Balthazar looked at the Revelator, to the bottles and pouches and dried parchments on the shelf, then to Melchior, contemplating.

"It is tempting, my friend, and you are cunning to suggest it, but the risks, considering our companions, are too great," Balthazar said.

"I understand," the Revelator said. "Perhaps then, I can help in other ways."

The Revelator pulled a dusty leather and copper box from the shelf.

"These will aid you along your path," he said. "When Magdalene was attacked in the village, I had wondered why her magicks were useless against the centurions attacking her. After I had brought her and the couple to safety, I went back to the centurions' bodies to find out why. I found, among others, this."

The Revelator pulled forth a silver chain, an amulet to be worn around the neck, from which hung an odd rune-scarred chunk of ruby quartz.

"A chimeric orb," Balthazar said.

"Used to counter magicks and the arts of psychic attack," the Revelator said. "They were no mere centurions. They were members of Herod's elite occult guard."

"So they were prepared against supernatural attack," Gaspar said.

"All the more intriguing and shocking," Balthazar said, "is that they were expecting it. Otherwise why not send standard centurions for what would appear to be a standard purge? Why risk his elite?"

"Exactly," the Revelator said. "Herod is an earthly king. He distrusts the spiritual. But in this instance, he has been in the counsel of seers and otherworldly aids all along, guiding him on this matter. Which means he knows of the import of this situation and the forces protecting his quarry. Otherwise he wouldn't have sent an elite cadre to what appeared to be a purge not unlike those he had ordered countless times past, whether at his violent whim or to wantonly exert his power."

"So what you are saying is that Herod is under sway of the dark arts and we should expect continued attacks along those lines, beyond even those of mercenary sub-demons like The Six?" Melchior said.

"Yes, and as you continue the attacks will increase in level, beyond those of earth-bound beasts like The Six," the Revelator said, "And you should likewise be prepared."

The Revelator explored the box further, revealing a series of amulets of runed silver and ruby chimeric quartz.

"The most vulnerable spots of a human to attack are the mind and the heart," the Revelator said. "I have fashioned these, forged and blessed them to be most potent in securing and protecting both. These align and fortify the defenses of those gateways and shield them from demonic devices."

He handed one to Balthazar.

"Mary and I wore amulets of this nature while battling The Six and they were mighty in warding off the demons' psychic attacks," the Revelator said. "Given, The Six were weak in the powers of the mind, their danger was greatest on the physical realm, but these should prove useful."

"Intriguing," Balthazar said.

"Not all demons have the power to invade the heart or mind but those that do…" the Revelator began.

They heard a clattering sound from upstairs. Balthazar turned to Gaspar.

Nearest the exit, Gaspar had already turned and was bounding up the stairs, to check on the man and woman, the Arimathean right behind him. Balthazar, Melchior and the Revelator sealed away the sacred artifacts and followed seconds behind.

As the latter three slipped through the secret entrance to the upper level, they noticed the doves in the cage agitated, but otherwise little of consequence. The Arimathean and Gaspar were sheathing their swords as Zechariah stood quizzically among them, his family and the couple in the other room, curious about the disturbance.

"Something must have rattled the doves," Gaspar said. "But it appears to be nothing."

"Appears," Balthazar said. He looked at Gaspar and the Arimathean and gave them a sign.

"We will stay here," Gaspar said.

Balthazar, Melchior and the Revelator walked back to the clandestine portal to the underground. The Arimathean and Zechariah were already in the main room as Gaspar, following behind them, heard something and spun quickly.

He noticed, slunk into a corner, two eyes shining, lurking in the shadows.

In instinct, his hand flew to his belt and a knife rose at the ready, halting as a black cat leapt from hiding and out the window past the frantic doves.

Gaspar breathed a heavy sigh.

Balthazar and the others returned to the room.

"What is it?" Balthazar asked.

"Nothing," Gaspar said, turning to Zechariah. "Your cat was sneaking about, probably hunting mice, or trying to get at the doves, and it almost became the hunted."

Zechariah looked at him.

"We do not have a cat."

Melchior looked at Balthazar, then Gaspar.

"What did it look like?" Melchior said.

"Jet black, gaunt, long-limbed, huge orange eyes. . ." Gaspar said.

The Revelator interrupted him.

"Where was it?"

"Here, in this room, slunk into the corner, looking out towards the main room and the portal downstairs. It leapt out the window the second I turned."

Balthazar and the Revelator exchanged a glance, and then looked to Melchior, whose eyes widened.

The Revelator nodded and retreated downstairs to grab various items off the shelf and place them intently into a soft leather pouch then returned and handed it to Balthazar, who slung it around his waist.

"Get the man and woman ready, we must return to the road and on to Bethlehem as quickly as possible," Balthazar said to Gaspar, then turned to Zechariah, "Your family may not be safe here. You have the day. Take what you need and find refuge for at least a moon cycle before even considering a return."

Zechariah nodded and called to his son, Matthew, who scurried to begin preparations.

"Why? What is it? What, was the cat an omen?" Gaspar said. "I am not as acquainted in these arts as you."

"Worse," Melchior said.

"A familiar," Balthazar said. "A spy. A manifestation. An animal possessed to be used as a mystical looking glass through eyes the color of flame."

"But who, here?"

"Herod's spies are legion, as are his officers, sergeants and seers," Melchior said.

Balthazar turned to Zechariah.

"Who is the Empire's authority in this region? Is he of the ancient craft?"

"Indeed he is, of the dark arts, a despicable, low-bellied sort," Zechariah said. "A viscous slime."

"And what is his name?"

"Pilate," he said. "Pontius Pilate."

TWENTY-FIVE

The sight and smell of the camp was enough to make even the battle-seasoned soldier's stomach molt.

He rode into their grounds, located in a craggy desert outpost just beyond a large town, in the guts of the day. The reek molding the wind with a venomous potency had assaulted him before he had even descended the final hill.

On the outskirts of the camp were an array of bodies and bones, most of which were in a state of decrepitude, from decomposition or having been half-eaten. The bones were strangled about in what seemed to be a perverted pattern. Bleached in the scalding sun they had taken on the look of a jagged gate circling the encampment of small tents, around which a number of corpses and pieces of the dead were arrayed.

Everywhere, flies and maggots bit and squirmed.

And all the more unsettling were the soldiers within, unkempt and ratty centurions, who appeared to be barely on the cusp of sanity, hollow-eyed creatures, gaunt and parasitic, openly sating their disgusting needs upon the dead.

The messenger was a jaded warrior, selected carefully for such an assignment. He was heavy with muscle and armor and skin leathered by the sun, with a ragged mane and thick facial hair about thin, beady eyes. He had seen several battles before, was hardened by an array of degradations viewed and partaken in upon the fields of war.

But this was beyond anything he had encountered.

For a moment, it gave him pause, made him consider turning, running from the assignment before him. However, he quickly reconsidered the futility of giving in to such temptation, given the reward promised him, and the consequences of his desertion should he fail this task.

As if emerging from nowhere, a tall, lithe figure swathed in black appeared shockingly at the fore of the camp, and met the messenger a distance before the largest tent.

"You are Q'uaa'ttoii?" the messenger said, descending from his horse.

The seer nodded.

Arrayed in airy, flowing robes stitched with gold and embedded with amethyst, his face a moonstone ivory and pink mapped with blue veins peering through his rice paper skin,

Q'uaa'ttoii appeared to float above the earth, over the blood and death strewn about.

He beckoned the man forward.

The messenger looked for a spot for his steed but was quickly stopped by the seer.

"Do not leave it, bring it to the tent," the seer peered about. "No telling what might happen if you left it."

The messenger nodded, and, pulling his horse slowly, walked with the seer.

"What manner of quest would involve such decadence?" the messenger said.

"Herod told you nothing of it?"

"Little."

"Thirty three years past, the stars began to array in unusual forms, making way for the arrival of a great king and like prophets to walk beside him," Q'uaa'ttoii said.

"Hence Herod's purges, yes, I know," the messenger said. "I have taken part in, and led, a few."

"But Herod was not alone in his preparations," the seer said. "Satan, too, was well aware of the celestial harbingers. And as such, he began to mark the way to destroy his enemies heralded to emerge, by creating an army against them."

"How?"

"Within the corridors of human power, there are many men, corrupt, who turn to the supernatural to achieve and maintain their means," Q'uaa'ttoii said. "These men were easily seduced by the promises made in exchange for their seed within demon succubae sent forth to them, to populate the planet with demonic halflings, who could otherwise not exist upon this plane without a human body, an anchor to tether them. They arrived en masse to wreak havoc and ultimately, Satan hoped, to help destroy the one men might call messiah."

"One of whom is…"

"Yes, but he is one of many. Was, one of many, before he methodically hunted down and destroyed the rest," the seer said. "The aftermath of which you see here. Madness and squalor, an army driven to its furthest depths, haunted by the psychic wounds and foul resonance of years of battling and slaughtering the unholy spawn of Satan."

"So those spawn are no more? All but the one I arrive for have been destroyed?"

"Aside from him, all but one, now, has been sent back to hell."

"And the one aside from him?"

"He will not find the one who remains, because I have been the engine to discover his kin, and I have my reasons, as you well know, to follow a different leader in this matter."

"Herod," the messenger said. "Herod has the other in hiding."

The seer nodded.

"So why did Herod allow the slaughter of the rest?" the messenger stopped just before they were to enter the main tent. He reached into a leather pouch slung about him and pulled out a glass tube, sealed at both ends, within which held a rolled scroll.

"To eliminate his competition," Q'uaa'ttoii said. "Which should come as no surprise, to you."

Q'uaa'ttoii stretched out an array of six spindly fingers and pulled the entrance of the huge tent aside, guiding the messenger in, into a strange chill, and a macabre, coal-black stillness.

The two entered the dwelling, the messenger's stallion remaining just inside its fold, and walked a few strange, disorienting steps in darkness, until, with a wave of Q'uaa'ttoii's hands it became illuminated, and the messenger doubled over, retching.

Strewn around the area in bizarre and awkward poses were a series of corpses, of all body types and ages, most of which were half-eaten and teeming with maggots. Some of them were cracked and bent as if seated in some strange arrangement around the figure in the center.

The only one alive.

He was a massive, brutal, muscular figure of shark belly skin, jagged and slimy armor that resembled the exoskeleton of an insect, slashed in cruel patterns and irregular spikes jutted at horrific angles. His dripping hair was like burnt oil, his eyes consumed with tremendous ebony pupils that seemed to hypnotically twist in turgid whirlpools, endlessly into the maw of hell. His nose and cheekbones were knife-like and unforgiving and his battle-scarred face was slickened with blood and gore, as he gnawed on a shank of human leg held wantonly in his gargantuan hands. He smiled with sardonic joy, his fangs glimmering with fresh blood.

The son of Herod and demon.

Herodius.

"It appears we have a guest," Q'uaa'ttoii said, slyly. "A messenger, from your father."

Herodius cackled and rose to greet the messenger, who had regained his composure.

"How terribly rude of me," Herodius said, gesturing around the tent to the bodies. "I should introduce you to my family. Especially as you and my father have already become acquainted. Look upon my brothers and sisters, are they not a lovely sight?"

"Yes, yes," the messenger said.

"Of course they are," Herodius purred, gently stroking the half-bone, half-flesh cheek of one of the corpses. "Lovely, so lovely."

Herodius turned to the messenger.

"Perhaps you will sup with us, tonight? I am certain they would enjoy your company."

The messenger nodded slightly, not wanting to appear rude.

"But, of course, that is a mere courtesy, and not why you have driven your," Herodius licked his lips, eyeing the beast at the gateway, "beautiful steed such a long way to meet with us, is it?"

The messenger slowly shook his head in the negative, then held out the glass with the scroll. "I bring word from your…"

"My loving father, yes, of course," Herodius said. "He must miss me so."

Herodius took the glass in his hands and lifted it, smirking as he looked it over.

He looked at the messenger, craning his neck and pursing his forehead with fake sincerity as he held the scroll out towards the man who had given it to him.

"Would you read it to me?"

The messenger halted, then looked to the seer, and back at Herodius.

"Please," Herodius said. "It would mean so much to me. Almost as if my father were reading it himself."

"I was, not ordered, I was told that only you could open the seal," the messenger said.

Herodius nodded.

"I am certain you were."

He placed the glass canister gently upon the lap of one of the corpses, which was twisted upward to resemble it being seated before him.

"Could you please hold this for me?" Herodius addressed the corpse. "Thank you, you are too kind."

The messenger and the seer traded glances.

"I am curious," Herodius said to the man. "How did my father know of my whereabouts? Has word of my exploits so quickly reached his kingdom?"

The messenger hesitated.

"Your father's eyes and ears are everywhere, my lord. His eyes are those of the raven and the asp."

"Yes," Herodius said. "There are a great many vermin and scavengers about the camp who resemble him."

The messenger gestured toward the glass.

"No doubt his pleasure over your triumphs is held within the scroll."

Herodius looked at the glass, then the man before him.

"I thank you, for your diligence and duty," Herodius said, looking at the messenger, and holding out his huge, dark claws for the man, as if offering him a gesture of graciousness.

The messenger tentatively reached out to take his hands.

With a bolt, Herodius grabbed both of the man's arms and snapped them, the bones shattered, leaving them dangling uselessly at his side.

The messenger howled in pain, and Herodius ferociously grabbed the man's red, wincing face, forcing his mouth to remain open, the man's tears streaming down onto Herodius' bloody hand.

"My father has wished me nothing but death since my birth," Herodius scowled. "Despite my efforts to rule beside him as rightful heir, he has been trying to kill me from the time I escaped my devil whore mother's womb. Why do you think I left his kingdom, upon this quest? He has had nothing but scorn for me, nothing but hatred, and I have nothing left but the same for him! And now, there is nothing of our accursed family, no one remains to challenge me but my cur of a father whose enslavement and death will be slow and torturous for all he has done to me. And then it will be he who shall live in fear and shackles and beg before my throne!"

Herodius grabbed the glass cylinder.

"My father loves nothing but power and chaos," Herodius scowled. "So I shall bring both to him with open arms."

Herodius spit blood upon the messenger's face.

"Here is my message to him," Herodius said. "You can deliver it when you greet him in hell!"

Herodius pulled the man's jaw open wide and brutally shoved the glass and scroll inside and down the messenger's throat, then slammed the man's mouth shut on it, as it shattered.

The broken glass caused the man to spasm and spew blood from his mouth. However, it was the poison, saturating the dissolving scroll, that made his body convulse violently about the ground before, only seconds later, it stopped, cold in death.

Herodius and Q'uaa'toii looked down upon the body, and Herodius, with a series of mighty kicks, sent it hurling from the tent to the scalding desert outside.

"You do not deserve to dine with us, or be dined upon by us," Herodius scowled as he pummeled the body from his lair. "Let the scum that follow me and my father's vermin devour you."

He looked to Q'uaa'toii.

"The last town, the last death, marked the final demise of my blood rivals to the throne?"

"There are none now, but Herod."

"You are certain?"

"Yes."

Herodius gritted his teeth.

"Then, my seer, we shall ride in return to the palace at dawn."

"I will alert the men."

"Wait," Herodius said, lifting the leg bone he had been devouring.

He clamped it hard in his jaw, chomping it and breaking it off sharply.

"First, I must exact revenge upon the one who betrayed me to my father."

"Of course," Q'uaa'toii said. "We shall find him and do so immediately."

"Indeed," Herodius said.

The seer turned, reached out his long, trembling hands to grasp and open the tent, then revolved slowly to Herodius.

"After you, my lord…"

With a vicious thrust, Herodius ran the spear of bone into Q'uaa'toii's chest, with such force his arm rammed through the seer's rib cage. Herodius kept his arm embedded in his betrayer, pulling the jerking body close as he sneered horrible curses into Q'uaa'toii's ear. Then Herodius, smirking, still looking into his seer's eyes, never wavering, yanked his spiked, armored arm back through the dead man's torso, leaving a huge, heaving void.

"Thank you, Q'uaa'toii," Herodius sneered. "How kind you are."

The seer's sunken body slumped to the ground.

Herodius kneeled to its side and spat in its face, then kicked it to the dust and sand outside his tent, alongside the corpse of the messenger.

He slunk back into the dwelling, smirking at the horse, which instinctively backed away in fear, just inside the entrance.

"So kind of my father to send me a fresh steed," Herodius sneered. "My last one just doesn't have the same life it used to."

Cackling, grinding his teeth and tasting the blood upon his lips and sneering, Herodius sat down, leaned back, and began licking the blood and meat dripping from his armor, as he laughed deeply.

And as the darkness once more fell in the tent, a fly began to buzz.

Louder.

Louder.

Louder.

TWENTY-SIX

The pilgrims traveled throughout the day, and as the sun was arching downward, rusting on the horizon and lacing the sky with an explosion of magenta and blood orange, the ground ahead of them grew hazy.

The warriors journeyed at the back of the caravan, expecting any attack to emerge from whence they came. And in the distance, framed against the setting sun, were the figures of Joseph and Mary, their horses galloping slowly along, the man vigilant beside his pregnant wife.

The Arimathean watched the two of them and as much as he loathed his heart for feeling anything but mercenary watchfulness, he allowed himself a moment of sympathy, of admiration, of, caring.

There had been too many signs, too many prophets, in his lifetime alone. Too many innocents, women and children, slain as a consequence, senseless victims of the paranoid delusions of men of power, who wanted to hold grasp of it in any way they could, regardless of their means of doing so.

Herod had been a particularly virulent enforcer of this psychotic creed, and the moment any of his endless string of dubious seers had dubbed an unborn to be a threat, there would be a mindless purge, followed by accusations and imprisonments and inevitable injustice.

He looked upon these two, Joseph and Mary, and saw two in love. About to celebrate the most beautiful thing he could think of upon this dirty, terrible, forsaken planet – the birth of a child who was truly adored, before it had ever set foot upon this world. But instead of it being a time of happiness and glory, it was a nightmare of uncertainty, which they spent not preparing for the blessed arrival, but instead running for their lives under the trust and protection of strangers.

All to flee the most base and primal brute instincts of a petty man flung through fortune into power.

Herod had done nothing to earn his prominence, and less to deserve retaining it. He was born, it was his. So went the fate of so many in similar seats of influence. They had done nothing to ascend to their places in the world, nothing but coast upon the good fates of fortunate birth. And yet they felt entitled to reign upon others. Why? And why were such men of low character and horrible ways given the honor of such station through lineage to begin? Or were they, too, innocent upon birth only to be turned, transformed, and corrupted by the power?

Why any man or messiah would wish to be born into this world was beyond him, the Arimathean thought. Even to fight to bring it justice. It would be best to leave this accursed world to die, to be forgotten, a good riddance to the universe.

He looked away from the couple and his countenance grew tenebrous, his eyes slanted and his forehead furrowed under the fiery storm of his mane and the wicked cut of his brow.

He shot a glance at Balthazar.

"So why these two? Why, amidst all the violence and death Herod is inflicting now, do these two and their child receive your protection?"

"I think you know, whether you wish to or not," Balthazar said, a slight smile accompanying his words.

"And I think you enjoy speaking in riddles a bit too much," the Arimathean smirked.

"Oftentimes," Balthazar said, "what you may deem a riddle is little more than my way of saying a question raised aloud is often one already answered within by one who is only seeking reinforcement of that he believes he already knows but is afraid to admit."

Balthazar chuckled.

"All I know," the Arimathean sighed, rolling his eyes, "is that you think this is another of your prophets that promise everything but deliver nothing but a swift death of martyrdom."

"If you would like to think of it that way, you may."

"Well, thank you for your kind permission, Balthazar."

Balthazar smiled gently as he watched the couple, their figures close together, riding alongside one another.

"I feel for them," the Arimathean said.

"You do?" Melchior said.

"I feel for them in getting caught up in your insane quest," the Arimathean said. "I feel for the infant and the expectations upon him. I feel for the parents, the child growing older, never being able to have a regular life. All of them, constantly feeling the weight of a people's fate upon them, the chains of a destiny that will likely reach a sad end. After all, your track record has not been too impressive. Pretty much all of your prophets have been killed, most of them publicly humiliated in death."

"Fate merely arrays the possibilities," Melchior said. "We all ultimately stride upon the paths we choose."

"Or that we feel obligated to choose," the Arimathean said. "Because from an early age we are given little choice otherwise."

"Perhaps," Balthazar said. "Perhaps. Or perhaps, they have come to this from beyond, fully knowing their fates, fully knowing that which God has in store for them. Here, and apart from this realm."

"I just wonder if these two, if their child, would not be far more happy living lives bereft of the fates for which you, or your God, have marked them?" the Arimathean said.

"We marked them not," Melchior said. "These are the ways of the heavens, we merely follow their course."

"Right," the Arimathean said, sighing.

"If you are so passionate a disbeliever, why do you risk your life in protecting those you disbelieve?" Gaspar said.

"Well," the Arimathean said, "I may not care about your mythical quests, but I likewise dislike the idea of women and unborns being killed."

He spat on the ground and looked into the horizon.

"Besides, I have my own reasons to hate the Empire."

"But those reasons, and your thirst for revenge driven by them, could have been executed long ago, without our aid," Gaspar said.

"Well, as you have astutely pointed out, and much as I loathe to admit it, I could have been executed as well," the Arimathean said. "Long before reaching the aim of my quest."

"Perhaps," Gaspar said. "Perhaps such lucidity created a delay in your vengeance. Or perhaps your travels could not locate your quarry? And perhaps you hope Herod's bloodlust and fear will eventually cause him to send the one you seek to attempt to slay the youngling and his mother?"

"Perhaps," the Arimathean sneered. "Perhaps."

"Perhaps?"

"You forget, I also trained under Balthazar," the Arimathean said. "I speak fluent riddle."

"Your cryptic answer only deflects the truth," Gaspar said.

"Or exposes it," the Arimathean said.

"So someone who espouses such selflessness is not so selfless after all," Gaspar said.

"Enough. It matters little, the motives seen and unseen," Balthazar said. "We have been pulled back into each other's orbit for good cause, beyond that which lies immediately before us, and which shall be revealed before long."

"Believe what you want, Balthazar, you always do," the Arimathean said.

"My friend, if you wished, and if it were fated, you would not be among us today," Balthazar said. "Yet you are, for good cause."

"I know you," the Arimathean said. "I figured it would be a matter of time before you found me. And yes, I also figured I could use that to my advantage."

"Call it what you wish," Balthazar said. "Fate knows many names."

"It is true," Melchior said. "There are some who would be of our order, if not for their own divergence from the path. But even their divergence is part of a larger tapestry."

The Arimathean looked at him, and Melchior nodded subtly to Mary and Joseph. The Arimathean looked at the pair.

"The man?"

"Everything happens for a reason," Balthazar said. "We all choose our paths, but in the greater universe, those paths may in fact be chosen for us to select from."

The Arimathean shook his head slowly.

"It makes little matter, it is nothing outside the realm of this world," he said. "The man is of the house of David, of relation to the sacred order. It only makes sense he would be chosen, or would choose, such a path. And likewise it would only make sense, according to the sacred writings, that you would choose them as a vessel for your faith, to elicit your protection."

"And what of your protection?" Melchior said.

"As I said, I have my reasons," the Arimathean said, "and they have little to do with your supernatural quests."

"So you say," Melchior said. "However, these reasons, your actions, have nothing to do with the beliefs you once held?"

"Once," the Arimathean said.

"And no more?" Balthazar said.

The Arimathean paused, looked at the couple in the horizon, off into the sky, then at Balthazar.

"What have your religious myths brought but false hopes and more reasons for hatred, divisions and war?" the Arimathean said. "None of these messiahs unites us or leads us against the true enemy. Every time a new alleged prophet is born, and inevitably dies in martyrdom, it gives birth to a new offshoot of faith. And each time another branch arises it gives the Empire one more way to divide us. As if they need any help."

The Arimathean gazed hard at the Magi.

"Give me a messiah with a sword to overthrow the Empire, to truly create a better world, and I will follow," the Arimathean said. "Until then I will walk my own path, blazed by the light of my own blade."

"And what compass of justice does it follow?" Melchior said. "That of man or God?"

"I do not need an invisible man in the sky, who may or may not exist, to tell me what is right and wrong. I can figure it out myself. Especially when His own sense of justice seems horribly askew."

"Have you never attempted to reach out to God again?" Gaspar said.

The Arimathean glared. "We're not exactly on speaking terms."

There was a long silence.

"God is not responsible for your misfortune," Melchior said.

"No?" the Arimathean countered.

"No," Gaspar said. "Herodius and his men killed your wife and children, ordered by Herod. And know this, my friend, that I can scarcely blame your thirst for revenge, and stand by your side in righteousness to see it executed. But you must know, they were hardly ruled by God in doing such a wretched deed."

"Perhaps," the Arimathean said. "But God did not do anything to stop it either, and if I was not away from them, off with you, protecting another one of your potential messiahs, dragging some woman and child off into the desert to hide them, I would have been there to stop it myself!"

"Maybe you would not have stopped it," Gaspar said. "Maybe He drew you away so that you would not be killed with them."

"He did me no favors then," the Arimathean said.

"Perhaps He did but you have yet to realize why," Melchior said.

"Why then? Why would my life be so much more important, when I would give it up willingly, in a second, for theirs?"

"Have you ever thought that God is acting through you, through us, to stop this? Have you considered that the birth of this child may have some impact on halting that violence?" Melchior said.

"When has it ever before?" the Arimathean snapped back. "How many messiahs have there been? How many prophets? How many supposedly great men to lead the tribes from exile, to lead the downtrodden against their constant oppressors, the elite that control their lives? Yet none have succeeded. Why do they even bother?"

"Have you ever asked why the people are so full of hope? Why they continue to believe?" Balthazar said. "Why do you think there are so many potential messiahs, as you say? Do you think it may be because there are so many who are looking for someone to follow? So many in need of hope and change and faith? Do you think it may be because so many hunger for something more in their lives?"

"If God is as powerful as you say, He could alleviate that hunger in an instant, without these charades," the Arimathean said.

"In time, my friend, in time," Balthazar said.

"Time, time," the Arimathean spat. "Who has time? The dead? Those dying every day as props in your crusades? If God is all-powerful, why not just stop the violence Himself?"

"Then what would be the purpose of free will?" Balthazar said.

"What is the purpose of free will now? To let the worst side of human scum reveal itself?" the Arimathean said. "To show that humanity is doomed to be nothing but a freak show of filth and horror until the day it thankfully is wiped from our planet? Free will! Free will! That is what you always fall back on, that is what you always talk about. If you ask me, free will is overrated. All it has done is given evil men the means to do horrible things."

"And good men the will to try to stop them," Balthazar said.

"To try, not always to succeed," the Arimathean said.

"Civilization survives because there are far more striving for good," Melchior said.

"And it suffers because their attempts too often end in failure," the Arimathean said.

They rode in silence, as the sun's last slivers of light clung to the horizon and slipped away.

"So then, why do you try?" Melchior said. "Why continue to battle, to stand for what you feel is right, when you could just as easily go down the other path, which would seem to be so much easier and more advantageous? Would that not seem to define your own faith, such as it stands?"

The Arimathean avoided the Magi's eyes, instead continuing to glance forward at the man and woman. The couple just ahead of their guardians, their soft laughter wafting back on a barely perceptible breeze to the men whose presence was a constant reminder of their peril.

In the sky above, the night fell like a cloak and the stars seemed all the more brighter, snaking down, brilliant and beautiful, from the light of the full moon.

"Faith," the Arimathean said. "Why serve faith when action is a far more satisfying master?"

TWENTY-SEVEN

Herod lounged, bored, in his torture chamber, watching slaves being ritually carved before him. As they were slaughtered, the blood of the slain was drained, through ancient onyx horns, into a massive gold chalice rippled with sigils and fiery cobra's eye gemstones, surrounded by spikes of flame. The blood had slowly begun to bubble and steam and Herod hungrily devoured the scent deep into his lungs.

Around the chalice, temple priests strode deliberately, murmuring in archaic tongues. They were dressed in spires of helmets with the faces of lions that spiraled down and around into tentacles down the back, above long violet robes licked with gold ropes swaying, laconically, like chains about their necks.

Emerging from behind a heavy curtain, Ozmondias scurried to Herod's side.

"Let me guess, more bad news?" Herod sighed.

Ozmondias bowed his head.

"The Six are no more. The One and his cadre continue unabated."

Herod's face smoldered tempestuously. He gripped the arms of his throne powerfully, trembled and growled, then released his grip, exhaling loudly.

He leaned over a cage of pristine white birds beside him and plucked one out, petting it softly and treating it as a tender lover. He breathed calmly, his chest expanding and dropping, cooing and coddling the tiny treasure until his countenance turned lighter.

He looked down to the bird, stroked its head gently and kissed it.

Then snapped its neck and tossed the corpse back into the cage, where the remaining birds enveloped it.

Ozmondias lowered his gaze.

"Leave me," Herod said. "Go to the oracles that also do me no service and attempt to save your pathetic selves, one last time."

Ozmondias bowed obsequiously and scurried from the room.

Herod brooded. The king slumped in his throne, drinking deep from his goblet, watched the servants being murdered and sardonically mimed their moans and cries of pain. He chuckled, but it brought him little of its usual amusement.

Then, within his left ear he began to hear it.

A slight buzz.

Then louder.

And louder.

And then he felt the tender stabbing of tiny, hairy, spiked feet upon his skin and he swung angrily about his head.

A fly buzzed around the dying slaves. At first, the flights seemed random and askew but eventually Herod noticed uncannily deliberate patterns about the bodies. As three more cried out upon expiring, the fly came to rest, lapping at the blood along the corners of the sacrificial chalice.

Its putrid purr grew louder, louder, louder, and the fly transformed into a bat-like creature before morphing into a wisp of black smoke, which further took shape into a shimmering mamba which slithered up to Herod's throne.

"Heeerrrrrrooooddddd…"

Herod looked at the snake, amused, and raised an eyebrow.

"If this is your attempt to delight me, Ozmondias, you may consider yourself saved for another day."

"Heeeeeeerrrrrrrrrrroooooooooodddddd….." the snake hissed. "Blooooooooooodddddd…."

Herod felt a chill grow over him, seeping up through his body into his head, a dark slime coating him, until at the base of his skull he felt a crackle and a slight buzzing sound in his ears. He felt a scratch about his face and flung his hand around to dismiss it, only to notice the snake was gone, and upon his hand was a huge, disgusting, hairy black fly, with the fangs of a lion and the eyes of a man. He attempted to shake it free but it would not yield, and instead, it dripped from its abdomen twelve small, light gray eggs upon the hand of Herod.

The king, filled with fear, tried to remove them, whipping his arm about in a frenzy, but, along with the fly, they remained, burning into his flesh. Herod's hand flung down upon his throne arm backward to crush the fly and its spawn. But it was to no avail. They remained unscathed. Unhindered.

The eggs burned twelve small ovals into the back of Herod's hand, drawing blood, which caused them to stain crimson, at which point they popped from Herod's flesh and flung into the sacrificial chalice, while the fly remained behind, still spiked to Herod's skin.

From its tiny maw it emitted a scratching sound that seemed almost a laugh.

"Herrrrrroooooodddddd...." The fly skritched, and then, with a wave of Herod's wrist, the insect was gone.

Herod breathed out heavily. He was caked in sweat, but a chill was upon him. Gooseflesh pimpled his girth as a freezing wind ripped through his palace.

However, despite the tempest, a dark cloud, hovering, hovering, hovering, remained just beyond his throne, unmoved by the torrent. It transformed, first into what appeared to be a human body, but one composed of the darkest, most acrid smoke, from which emitted a vomitus array of pus-filled and bloody wounds and boils, a mass of strange eyeballs of all shapes and sizes.

From amidst the pile of stench and ruin, one eye, like that of a reptile, a bleeding, green and crimson slit, burst forth. It burbled from the top of the perverse form and the murk around it coagulated into what appeared to be a head on the smog beast. Beneath the eye seeped forth a mouth, like that of an ancient, just before death, toothless and bare, with a tongue forked like a snake's.

Herod was shocked for a second but regained himself.

"What manner of being are you and what do you want? Blood? More blood? And what is more, how can you aid me, in exchange for the blood you seek?"

The being coughed and cackled a creaking laugh that made the gooseflesh on Herod once more erect along his entire body.

"You know my name, in the number of a man, for it is a human number, six-hundred-and-sixty six…"

Herod's eyes grew wide.

"Satan," he said. "So you have finally arrived."

"Then you know why I have come, how I have traveled to this world, through the blood and pain you have spilled to invite me. The six-hundred-and-sixty-six souls you have drained for me."

Herod composed himself.

"What is it you seek?"

"The same as you, the death of the new king. The death of the Christ. But not a human death. A death all the more. A death of the soul."

"A death of the soul?"

"Simple Herod, you are but a man, a man for whom death is a death of the body, a death of the flesh. But if you kill the host, the woman whose flesh houses the Christ, in ritual, and rip from it the bloody unborn, the power of the child can be claimed and chained. In ritual, it shall be bound and mine."

"It can be?"

"The unborn and its host. Alive. Have your emissaries, our emissaries, deliver the woman and unborn to you, to me, and upon ritual we shall make a sacrifice. The blood will be spilled, slowly, the bodies shall remain unburied and unburned. The infant shall be ripped from the mare and christened in blood and fire. And the power within, the baby unborn, shall be no Christ. Instead he shall be, Anti-Christ."

Herod's eyes glimmered with malevolence.

"And he shall rule upon this planet and you by his side, and we shall manifest. I, into this world, for a millennium, will rule, and even beyond, if we shall turn it to our side, away from the God, and instead to a world of our making."

Herod smirked.

"The unborn," Satan hissed, "ripped from the womb, bloody and untouched, and the woman's heart, torn still beating from her breast, as sacrifice, upon the bodies of a thousand slaves, still and sweated, burned and bloody, as its throne. The ritual shall make it so. The Christ, shall be, Anti-Christ. For it is ordained. For so it is foretold."

Satan began to burn, the bleeding, seeping wounds dripping from his wall of acrid smoke dripping sticky gloops of muck upon the floor, and Herod bared his fangs, his eyes alight.

"I must find a manifest to anchor in this cursed place," Satan growled. "Herod, look to me!"

Herod stared into the darkening, nightmarish fog, and his mind froze, expanded and snapped, then sharpened, then began to become eclipsed, possessed. His body stiffened, then began to shake, and his eyes rolled back and went white and the mists of Satan engulfed him, seeped into Herod's pores and every orifice, until the human's body was in the demon's grasp.

The Herod/Satan symbiotic called Ozmondias and a cadre of centurions, and they were told to collect twenty-three slaves, stripped bare and stretched on a stone altar placed before them.

Into their flesh, intricate runes and ancient epithets were carved, and before the demon-human abomination they lay bleeding, upon inverted pentagrams of ash and blood and silver shards and occult oils and weeds, ripped and thrown upon them.

As the chants of the monks about them dulled and the light of the candles faded away, the sacred blades fell, and the cries and the begging and the sobs of the dying filled Herod's palace. He did nothing but laugh, his eyes burning, his skin throbbing and oscillating with the beast now within him.

When at long last the final breath was dropped from a servant's lips, Herod/Satan had the soldiers seize his stunned and pleading seer, and they held Ozmondias down onto the altar.

"Ozmondias, you have failed me in life," Herod/Satan purred, "perhaps your otherwise worthless shell shall find a purpose in death."

The seer attempted to battle for his life, using all of his unearthly powers, but they were nothing against the power of Satan, flowing through Herod, which neutered the seer and quickly subdued him for the soldiers.

Chaining Ozmondias down, they carved upon his sallow skin the most foul sigils of all, the most putrid curses and spells. As the last of twenty-three knives descended upon him, bursting his heart, the demon Satan left Herod's body in a black ooze and the murky being grasped the last breath of Ozmondias and hurtled it back into the former seer's chest, devouring it and slithering into the dying host's mouth, causing the pale, bloody body to jerk and explode at obscene and disturbing angles, the eyes of Ozmondias no longer there, now replaced with aught but black, the darkest shark eyes, sheer and endless, with nothing but the distant spark of Satan's fire, deep inside them.

With the utmost evil made manifest in the world, he raised his hands and growled and thrashed like a wild animal in words unheard since the birth of time, calling forth demons to rise from the blood of the fallen, to hatch from the eggs he had spewed upon the earth, supping upon the blood of Herod and the sacrificed.

A foul smell infested the throne room and pestilent piles burbled from the blood and gore upon the floor, until they rose, as a phalanx of twelve.

Twelve demons so wretched as to cause most men to vomit and go insane instantly at the mere sight of their bodies. Translucent dead flesh stretched across a scabbed and awful land of bursting pus, infected wounds and rippling faces shrieking through scenes of horror and debauchery stretched tight beneath their skin, whirling beneath their scaled, see-through reptilian forms. And at their faces were eyes of a dragon and teeth of lions but the lips and features of the most beautiful of women, but beaten and scarred and horrible, hair matted and torn, jutted by horns and spikes ripped through skin and faces half shorn by cruelties, belied by their fanged smiles.

The V'nag'thi-hkai.

The soul rapers.

The twelve appeared before Herod, and the body of Ozmondias, his split and swollen flesh now occupied by Satan in whole, little more than a zombie, a marionette of rancid meat. And the demons bowed, looking upon him, their reptilian eyes meeting, and knowing.

What they were to do.

Where they were to go.

What they were to return.

The unborn, untouched, brought back to Herod and Satan.

Along with the mother, alive, for now, with her warm, wet, beating heart, to be kept alive by sorcery, if necessary.

Kept alive.

Until it would be no longer needed.

TWENTY-EIGHT

Balthazar awoke with a start, the last wisps of a dream's warning dissipating with the rapid pounding of his heart jolting his eyes alight. It was just before dawn and the sky had begun to glimmer in the distance. Seeping about the encroaching light like tentacles, streams of strange shadow licked and lashed against the sky.

Melchior had already woken and was readying for them to flee, throwing enchantments to pull the tents quickly, fading them to a mist that soared into a pouch on his belt.

"You had the dream as well?" Balthazar said.

Melchior nodded. "The omens have yet to deceive us."

The rest had likewise awoken and the group returned quickly to the trail, but it was to little avail as an encroaching wind had caught them, and with it a fog that became oppressive and dank.

Above them, the sky swirled dark and thick, like the heavy legs of a spider closing around its prey. Sickly green veins of lightning slithered about the clouds and burning hail began to pelt them, causing them to dash for cover in a rocky outcropping.

Balthazar and Melchior were chanting rapidly in unison, raising their arms to the sky, blue fire darting from their fists and into the heavens, causing the hail to immediately ash in an arc about their shelter, protecting them.

In the sky above them, Balthazar and Melchior noticed the otherworldly veins of green had begun to thicken, rivers of bile and blood across the blackened clouds, throbbing and crashing, until tearing open a horrible slit in the firmament.

"I do not like the looks of this," Gaspar said.

"Who would?" the Arimathean added.

The four men walked from the ragged impromptu shelter, leaving the couple behind. The Arimathean turned to Joseph and Mary.

"Stay here," he said. "No matter what."

The men watched as the rift grew to resemble a huge eye, and from it, a dozen jet black reptilian pupils, thin and sharp, emerged. The stains grew larger, larger, until they could be discerned as demons horrible and gruesome, flapping towards them on wings that broke the heavens with a sickening squishing and an awful stench that began to permeate the air.

"Are those what I think they are?" Gaspar said.

"The V'nag'thi-hkai," Balthazar said.

"The soul rapers," Melchior added.

"Who?" the Arimathean asked.

"Demons of an unholy level, only able to be summoned through the ritually-spilled blood of six-hundred-and-sixty-six hearts run through when poisoned with fear, under command of Satan himself," Balthazar said. "Those killed by their hand are condemned to the lower levels of hell to be defiled repeatedly for 1,000 years."

"Well, at least it's not 1,001," the Arimathean said.

"Yes, now that would be truly awful," Gaspar added.

"And what of their kind killed by our hand?" the Arimathean said, drawing his sword. "What hells do they face?"

"Mortal weapons cannot harm them," Melchior said.

"Great," the Arimathean said, sheathing his sword.

"But these can," Melchior said.

Melchior threw aside his cloak and revealed a midnight blue pouch stitched in gold. From it he pulled four small wands, looking like sword handles without the blades. They were shimmering ebony and dark greens and reds, like the backs of beetles, crawling with silver runes, an ancient language of curves and sigils, interspersed with interwoven stars.

Melchior held one in his right hand and uttered a brief prayer – two short, severe, steadfast lines in the old tongue – and the handle grew warm in his hands, surrounding his fist in a glowing symbol, four triangles crossed in disjointed paths, and from them emerged a glowing, brilliant, silver blade awash in iridescent runes that shimmered like moonstone.

Melchior handed the other three wands to Balthazar, Gaspar and the Arimathean and they followed suit.

"The Lok'Feign," the Arimathean said, glancing in admiration upon the blade in his hand.

"The legendary sacred swords of S'iam B'ala," Balthazar said. "Able to disrupt the auric fabric of all beings, leaving most humans stunned and asleep, but decimating the bonds tethering demons and lesser beings to this world, sending them back to the hell from whence they came, never to emerge again."

Balthazar looked heavenward to the soul rapers, gelling into formation, drawing ever near, and, around them soaring high above, a swirling of ravens.

He nodded towards the birds and then to Gaspar and Melchior.

"The eyes of demons are everywhere," Melchior said, eyes squinting at the growing mass of black crosses in the darkening skies.

"You mean the eyes of Pilate," Gaspar said, sword drawn and rising upward.

"What is the difference?" the Arimathean said.

The demons began to descend, and at last the warriors could see their fearsome visages, the exploding pustules, the bleeding teeth and eyes, the parchment skin which whirled like a turgid cesspool.

And when their mouths opened, a high pitched stabbing sound filled the air, and the Magi felt at the base of their skulls a slurping compression and a cracking sound like an eggshell being slowly crumpled.

As the crackling grew, it felt like tiny fingers were wriggling into their brains, like maggots bursting from a bloated corpse. And as the worms spread through their minds, the men's guts sank and the vague outlines of people and places began to form in their minds. Pictures of hellish chambers and depraved beasts and humans being led at knifepoint into the gore-soaked rooms, people stripped naked whose faces slowly morphed into those of their loved ones.

Only Balthazar, the most powerful and pure of the Magi, already carrying a chimeric orb about his neck, was resistant to the attack, but he sensed the onslaught and quickly took action to staunch the damage to his fellow warriors.

"Quickly, the Revelator's amulets!" Balthazar called to his companions, as they struggled to pull the strange ruby quartz necklaces over their heads and around their necks. And as they did, the demonic debasements dissipated, the voices of perversion fading away.

The psychic attack thwarted, the demons frothed and frenzied in frustration, and with claws and fangs bared, they surrounded the four and the man and woman among the rocks, and with a spine-shredding shriek, they stabbed downward in unison upon them in a frenetic blood lust, hissing, hissing to their prey.

"For a millennium of pain, you shall be ours."

TWENTY-NINE

Steeling themselves amidst a jungle of slashing talons and clashing fangs, the four battled fiercely to keep the demons at bay. Not content to slice and slash at the men's flesh, the reptilians continued to stab psychically at the warriors, attempting to weaken and overwhelm them. However, the protection stone amulets of the Revelator thwarted all but the feeling of pinpricks at the base of the men's skulls. Any invading perversions ejaculated into their psyches by the demons were disintegrated.

However, that did naught to stem the physical threat. The beasts from above attacked with speed and ferocity, in unison, three to a man, never tiring, never stopping as they whirled in, blades and claws and teeth and fury slashing.

Before long, the four men were lashed and bloody, but still they fought on, the sacred swords cutting wide swaths about them, taking their own sections of unholy flesh in return and keeping the demons at bay.

Balthazar's sword was first to claim demon life, as one of the hellions attempted to make a killing blow, only drawing itself in tight enough for Balthazar's blade to slice through it cleanly, leaving the two parts tumbling in separate directions, burning up in a repellent burst of smoke and being dispatched back to the lower hell from whence the demon had been summoned.

Melchior quickly followed with another kill, decapitating a demon which had attempted to tear the Mage's head from his shoulders but left its own neck vulnerable to the same fate.

The Arimathean drew third blood, not only stabbing through the heart of another demon, but sending its body, still burning on his sword, into the relentlessly attacking maws of his companions.

Gaspar did likewise, burying his sword arm deep up to his elbow in the chest of another demon, and fortunately escaping death as the beast had used its own demise to draw close enough to bite deep into the Magi's armor, light under his robes, tearing a chunk of sacred metal and slashings of flesh from Gaspar's shoulder as the demon dissipated.

Another attacked as Gaspar's arm was buried deep in his first kill but the advancing demon was stunned by the strength and speed of the Magi. Gaspar grabbed it by the neck, and kept it at distance while withstanding whiplash slashings of claws at him before his holy sword carved through the demon, cutting it in two as Gaspar hurled the disintegrating, whirling, flaming corpse at the third demon attacking him, blinding the unholy beast for just a moment, an instant in which Gaspar ran his sword up through it, exploding it in tar, bile and flesh.

Gaspar looked to his companions.

Empowered by the Revelator's amulet, which seemed to make him all the more formidable, Balthazar fended off repeated attacks, dodging and weaving through them, before planting firm and hurtling the demons back with a whirlwind of mystical icy shards. The frothing, furious beasts regrouped and frenzied upon him again but the Magi threw potent incantations to freeze the two remaining demons, dispatching them with a hurricane scythe of his sacred sword.

The Arimathean was unable to be seen, caught behind the rocks sheltering Joseph and Mary, and so Gaspar joined Melchior in fighting the pair of demons which had succeeded in slicing two long, ugly wounds into Melchior's chest armor and reducing his protective cloak to tatters.

Into the fray Gaspar leapt, and with the element of surprise managed to reduce Melchior's opposition to one, which found itself between the two Magi, where the demon soon found its doom, shouting vile epithets as it was destroyed.

Balthazar glanced at his companions and then strove to find the Arimathean through the Hadean mists that had risen around part of the battlefield. He heard a cry of terror – the woman – and flew into the morass swirling about the rocky shelter where the couple had fled.

When the attack had commenced from above, the four warriors had positioned themselves strategically around the couple's shelter, each taking a quarter, preventing the demons from attacking it directly, but it wasn't long before they had been forced away from their positions. Soon into the battle a demon managed to sail overhead and tear a rock above the couple completely from its mooring, exposing Joseph, huddled over Mary, his body covering hers in an attempt to protect her as they pushed themselves deeper into the tight space remaining in the crevice.

The Arimathean had found himself alone as their guardian, battling furiously while attempting to likewise watch over them, but with each attempt to parry a demon attack upon the couple, he left himself exposed, and soon his wounds were numerous.

His body was pocked with crimson slits, and the demons kept drawing closer, closer, as his sword's arcs grew slower, slower. His reactions more and more dull, with every chunk of flesh taken from him. The darting demons were relentless, attacking and fleeing, like wolves upon larger prey, inflicting death by a hundred wounds, slowly and surely.

He whirred quickly about the man and woman, protecting them like an animal cornered, his sword flailing about to stop the demons' sinister slicing, barely deflecting one, only to feel the other stab into him from behind, as he whirled about to turn a potentially killing blow into a glancing one as the demon retreated from the point of his sword. When it seemed as if the Arimathean was gaining an advantage, an attack would be made upon the couple, distracting the warrior and allowing one of the demons to exploit his vulnerability and exact another piece of flesh from the outmatched guardian.

But the Arimathean's time was short, and his mind began to leave him, his knees began to buckle, as he huddled in closer to Joseph and Mary, and the demons cackled in glee, thick spools of drool falling from their mouths in anticipation of the kill.

With a final, frenetic frenzy they hurled themselves at the Arimathean, but as the man lifted his sword weakly, expelling the final vestiges of his strength into the defense of the man and woman, making one last valiant stand, he found his sword instead passing through fiery ash, as the two demons had been slashed in half in midair, returned to hell by the swords of Gaspar and Balthazar.

The Arimathean, stumbling and swaying, a mass of blood and sweat, felt his arms grow heavy, the holy sword falling to his side. He looked back at Joseph and Mary.

"Are you alright?"

They nodded to him and his scowl lightened, his face unpursed and what appeared to be a slight smile crossed his lips, and then, his eyes closed and he fell, hard, to the ground, and his breathing slowed, slowed and drifted away.

THIRTY

Mary and Joseph got up and went to their champion's side, Mary attending to the Arimathean, her hands touching his sweaty, blood soaked face and matted hair, grasping his wrist, straining to feel a pulse.

"He is barely there, barely alive," Mary cried. "We cannot let him die this way! He gave his all to save us!"

Balthazar's long fingers cupped around her shoulder and she looked up at his kind visage, stepped aside as the Magi knelt down over the Arimathean's quivering body, growing colder, colder.

"Is he?" Gaspar said.

"Not yet, he's struggling, but..." Balthazar said.

"We cannot let him fall, subject him to..." Melchior said.

Melchior looked at the fallen warrior and breathed deeply, then knelt and put his hands over the fading face of the Arimathean.

"But surely you can heal him," Gaspar said. "Melchior?"

Melchior's eyes rolled back, his body began to quake, and an invisible force threw him from the body of the Arimathean.

"Melchior!" Gaspar rushed to help him up.

Melchior panted to catch his breath, wiping sweat from his brow.

"They have him."

"No!" Mary called out, weeping into her hands as Joseph put his arms around her.

"There is…nothing you can do?" Gaspar struggled forth.

"He is already more than half gone," Melchior said. "Victim to wounds of body and soul beyond even my power. The V'nag'thi-hkai are too strong beyond this realm, they… have his soul, and are dragging it down, despite his struggle."

Mary wept loudly, turning to Joseph and burying her head in his chest, as he placed his arms around her.

Balthazar looked to them, then to the other Magi, then to the putrid green lightning, oscillating, flickering, about the fading wound, the gaping maw, in the sky.

The portal between worlds.

Balthazar pulled the pouch from around his shoulders and handed it to Melchior.

"There is only one way to save him," Balthazar said.

The three looked at one another.

"Balthazar…" Melchior said.

"There is no other way," Balthazar said.

The most powerful of the Magi stood at full, outstretched his arms and looked to the gate still a fading whirlpool in the heavens.

"Quickly, Melchior, the holy items the Revelator gave us! Align them, trace them into the earth, to set the spell, the prayer, to keep the gate open, for as long as you can! Gaspar – construct a shield of protection so that we may be the only things entering or leaving this realm!"

Balthazar steeled himself, gathering his strength as he focused on the portal. Melchior and Gaspar pulled items from the bag and rapidly set them about in sacred sigils and runes and a halo began to form, alighting from the heavens and around them, and up to the bleeding bile green gateway.

"The only way of saving him is in the space between worlds," Balthazar said, looking at Melchior.

"But Balthazar, we know not where this pathway leads; only that it bled demons," Melchior said. "For all you know it leads to hell itself."

Balthazar looked at the gate, then to the Arimathean's unmoving body, then to Mary.

"Then I shall go to hell itself to save him," Balthazar said. "And I shall have to rely on my faith and the power of God to protect us, and bring us back."

With the icons and holy items in place, Gaspar and Melchior began to utter ancient prayers, growing in intensity and volume as they repeated them.

"How will you..." Joseph said.

"He is not yet completely gone, his body remains an anchor to his spirit," Balthazar said. "The one will guide me to the other, and it will act as a magnet for its return as well. I will take him and return him whole, or neither of us shall return at all."

"But Balthazar," Gaspar said. "It took the four of us to defeat them upon this plane, how will you alone do it on the astral plane beyond?"

Balthazar looked into his eyes.

"I will."

"How can you?" Gaspar said. "Their power is tenfold beyond this realm!"

"As is mine, Gaspar," Balthazar said, smiling slyly. "As is mine."

"But..."

"I have faith," Balthazar said, looking at Mary and Joseph. "And that will be enough."

Balthazar's arm looped around the Arimathean's limp, dying body, and pulled it to his side, dragging it along with him beneath the portal. He whispered soft prayers, his eyes closed, his head bowed, and the portal began to descend, slowly, toward them, stopping and starting, as if the portal were lowering against its will, as if it were being forced, by the Magi.

Balthazar's chants gained in volume and intensity, until finally the portal was before them, oscillating and glowing, seemingly struggling to free itself, as Balthazar girded himself to leap into it with the body of his friend.

He turned to his fellow Magi.

"Melchior, keep the portal open as long as possible. Gaspar, maintain the shield of protection and make sure nothing gets through that should not enter this world."

"And what if you do not return before the portal falls?"

Balthazar did not answer, only clenching his teeth, girding himself, and making a last look back at Joseph, then at Mary.

In her head, she heard a whisper, his voice, calm and reassuring. She listened, felt the weight of his words, and nodded to him.

Balthazar turned to Gaspar and Melchior.

"A great man once said to me, `Everyone dies. If there is any honor in this world, any glory, it is in giving your life to someone who deserves it.'"

He turned towards the entryway to the netherworlds, his eyes beginning to spark and glow a low blue, his body crackling with energy, as he took the Arimathean in his arms, holding him tight, and leapt into the open gate, and with a quicksilver cyclone explosion of energy they disappeared into it.

And in the putrid ochre of the storm's remains, the sky overcast and murky, the eerie window to the unknown snapped and hummed, emitting bolts of plasma that decreased in fury and potency as Melchior strained, strained, to keep the rift alive as it shrunk.

Smaller.

Smaller.

Smaller.

THIRTY-ONE

Sawdust danced gently in the fading daylight as the Arimathean set down his tools and looked over his day's work.

He caressed his hand along the curves of the small bed, then, stopping, he removed his calloused paws and gently, deliberately, ran the more sensitive inside of his forearm over the polished wood, feeling nothing but a reassuring smoothness.

He smiled and raised his arm to wipe the sweat from his brow.

Pulling it away, his eyes were drawn to the rugged, scowling mark of pallor creeping along the sun-bronzed map of his arm. He examined the scar and it was as if he could feel, again, the harsh talon tearing through his sinew and flesh.

Seven years.

It had been seven years now.

He felt the hairs on his neck stand a bit, and immediately he sensed a presence, an aura, behind him, approaching on tip-toe feet, stalking him.

His face brightened.

He heard a small scratch as a pebble was kicked, but he feigned obliviousness.

And with a hearty laugh and a massive bound, his two-year-old son grabbed his legs from behind, giving him a tremendous hug.

The Arimathean laughed and pretended to be surprised.

"Oh! You got me!" he said, as the boy giggled.

The Arimathean turned and pulled the toddler up into his arms, exposing the boy's belly and tickling it, then raining kisses upon his cheeks, holding him close as the two entered their home. He held the boy tightly and nuzzled his nose next to his, looking into his eyes. The boy was a mirror of him, olive skinned, a ripe berry of the sun, dark haired and with uncannily crystalline and vibrant eyes, the color of sienna brushed with gold, the earth at sun's set.

"Father!"

Two older children, a boy and a girl, with the darker skin and deep brown hair and eyes of their mother, leapt toward him and embraced the Arimathean. His wife, tall and beautiful, with delicate cocoa features and smooth skin and hair that made her look as though she was an ancient sculpture brought to life, walked to him and kissed him. He put his hand gently to her face, framing it as he looked into her eyes, then kissed her again.

His hand moved to the small curve of her belly and they smiled.

"Dinner is ready, I will finish setting the table while you clean up," his wife said.

"Thank you," the Arimathean said.

He set down his son, kissing him again and watching as the toddler joined his siblings running about the yard and into their home.

The Arimathean put his hand to his scruffy auburn beard, pausing a moment to gather the joy of the children at play, and walked back outside and picked up his work space for the night.

Placing the last tool back in its hold, he looked over at a dusty chest, locked and sealed. Walked to it, examined the dirt and film collected upon it, then pulled a small key from his belt and opened it.

He reached in.

Felt the leather upon his hands, the smooth steel of the hilt, the soft suede and the silky cold of the jewels embedded in it.

In an instant he was back on the battlefield again, the sounds and scents, the boiling adrenaline all hitting him in a relentless series of waves.

Reverently, contemplatively, he pulled the belt out of the chest. He looked down at his carpenter's wares, incongruously camped amidst the leather slung about him, and removed his work satchels, placing them down on his bench.

He looked again at the second belt, a warrior's tools, wrapped it around his waist and fastened it.

It felt heavy, foreign, unwelcome to him.

At first.

However, it only took a few seconds, and then, a drumbeat began to build in his chest, his blood began to crest, and his powerful hand clasped around the hilt of steel, felt it warm to his touch, and he felt the fire once again.

He sighed.

Removed his hand from the steel.

Considered a moment.

Then began to unfasten the belt, to return it to its place.

And stopped.

The Arimathean felt a presence, approaching behind him, sensed a magnetism, an aura of power with which he was all too familiar.

He smirked, and with uncanny speed and unerring aim, he jolted his sword from its scabbard, whirled around and caught the blade looming silent behind him. With a quick, clean jerk he spun it about and out of the hand that held it, sending the weapon sailing and impaling the ground beyond his visitor's reach. Then just as quickly, the Arimathean pulled a knife with his other hand and placed it blade up at the neck of the man standing before him.

Smiling widely.

"Balthazar," the Arimathean said, grinning and sheathing his weapons. "I knew it was you."

The two men embraced, as Melchior and Gaspar likewise stepped forward to greet the Arimathean.

"Your skills remain impressive, my friend," Gaspar said, "even after these many years."

"The senses of battle may be dull with lack of use," the Arimathean said, "but they have not completely disappeared."

"It is good to see," Melchior said.

"Yes," the Arimathean said. "Although the need for them has considerably diminished."

"Such was the case, my friend," Balthazar said. "No more."

The Arimathean felt his heart crash in his chest. He raised an eyebrow.

"A mission?"

"Indeed," Melchior said.

"We understand that you have found a peace, and happiness suits you very well, my friend," Balthazar said. "We would not ask were this not of incredible import."

"I understand," the Arimathean said. "But what is good for the world outside will only lead to good for our world here."

The Magi nodded.

"Walk with us, my friend," Balthazar said.

The four men strode to the outskirts of town, and as the dusk closed around them, the Magi unwound the quest that would begin when the sun returned. They plotted and planned as the day faded, before finally heeding the calls of the Arimathean's wife and returning to his home, to adjourn for the night.

They woke just before dawn and readied themselves, bidding their farewells to their hosts. The Arimathean embraced his brothers and friends, kissed and held his wife and children.

"I love you," he said, looking deep into his wife's eyes, liquid with concern.

He kissed her, held her tight and looked into her eyes again.

"Do not worry," he said. "I will see you soon."

"I love you."

"I love you too."

He mounted his horse. The Magi waved farewell and turned, spurring their steeds on. But the Arimathean lingered, for just a moment.

It had been a long while since he had been away. He knew he would miss his family horribly. But this was beyond that. He did not know why, but he felt something, beyond love, beyond longing, beyond a parting sorrow, that dug into his soul.

He felt compelled, to pause, to linger, to collect the image before him, of his family and loved ones.

He felt a sense of dread he could not explain, and for a moment he hesitated, saying a silent prayer that he would return, alive and safe, to his home. To his wife. To his children. And to their baby soon to arrive.

His eyes locked in embrace with his wife's. He looked upon her beautiful face, dark skinned, with full lips and a cascade of silken chestnut waves down around her smooth cheekbones and caressing her back, her figure full and warm and gorgeous.

He smiled softly, then turned away, spurring his horse on, on, as he rode into the distance to his fate.

The last thing he saw, just a flicker, as he turned to leave, behind him, was his youngest son, watching as his father faded, the boy raising a small blanket above his head and waving it, desperately and lovingly, to the man he had just held, so tightly.

The Arimathean could not bear to turn, to show the looming tears in his eyes. Instead, he held in his heart the image, the final visages, of his wife, beautiful and loving, standing against the sun. His boy, waving goodbye.

He held them tightly.

Tightly.

He did not know why at the time, only that he felt compelled to do so.

But he would find it was a cruel joke, an irony, that he would cherish that moment so potently, for it would be the last moment of happiness he would have.

And, therefore, it would become his greatest remaining joy as well.

It was that moment, that bittersweet but inescapably powerful moment of bliss, that Balthazar plucked from the mind and heart of the Arimathean.

The mighty wizard couched it like a delicate hatchling, gently in his hands, and wrapped it, warm and enveloping, around the dying man like a cloak. It haloed about him, a shield, to ward off the onslaught of demon bile and unimaginable evil around them, as they began their descent down, down, down into the bowels of hell.

Down, down, pulled by the strengthening chains lashed about the fading vestiges of the Arimathean's mortality, the binding curse of the V'nag'thi-hkai, which inexorably sucked the dying man's soul ever closer, closer, into the spiny jaws of their virulent wombs.

Razor sharp teeth, tiny splinters of solid fetid waste, began to hurtle upward at the two men as they descended, and from the murk, the creatures began to appear, slathering and obscene, readying themselves to partake of earthen souls and human flesh.

The demons prowled hungrily about them.

Balthazar clenched his teeth, held tight to the fading body of his friend, and girded himself for the battle ahead.

Holding his own anchor to the world, to hope, to faith, tightly about the two of them.

THIRTY-TWO

As the last of the V'nagh'thi-hkai had been slain, banished from earth and sent hurtling back to Hades by the sacred swords of the Magi, Satan's visage erupted in flame, blistering the skin of its once-human shell. His voice shrieked in frustration, shaking Herod's temple to its foundation and slathering gooseflesh among all who heard it.

"They have failed!"

Herod sat uneasy upon his throne.

The travelers live on?"

"Two of their champions have been spent, but the woman and spawn remain unstopped on their journey!"

Herod composed himself, his forehead beading with sweat as he watched the wretched body once occupied by his vizier shudder and thrash, rip its already scarred, scabbing skin and grit its teeth with such force as to shatter and shard them into spikes.

"The time grows near, the heavens align, and they shall be in safe haven," Satan said. "If they traverse the grounds of this unholy night into the day we will find ourselves with few opportunities hither to deliver them to death or possession."

"Few or none?" Herod said.

"Two years hence, the heavens will misalign in retrograde, allowing a window in which the child and mother can be slain," Satan replied. "But then not again for thirty-one years, as it has been written."

"What demons, then, to avail against them to bring us the unborn and his mother's heart still beating, before the heavens turn against us?" Herod said.

Satan paused, his sentience slashing across the metaphysical pathways, between the dimensions and through a wormhole across the earth, into an avian familiar, miles away, floating above the travelers.

Upon his presence's arrival in the black-winged, earthly shell, the sky rent asunder, ripped by the intrusion of the high demon back into the earthly plane, and a bolt of lightning stabbed through the clouds to scorch the earth. Through the raven's icy vacuums he watched, soaring from above, as Melchior and Gaspar strained to maintain the gate.

With a heaving pull, Satan withdrew his essence from the familiar, and back across the astral transom to the misshapen shell of Ozmondias. His jagged teeth smiled and he laughed with a hacking cough, deeply and mockingly.

"They leave the gate alive, and what is more struggle to keep it open, the means to their own destruction. And through it, their bodies will be boiled and their minds and souls defiled and impaled in hate for all eternity."

"And who shall lead this onslaught, by demon or man?" Herod said.

"Already I summon the means to their destruction, by demon claw and fang shall they suffer for all eternity," Satan growled.

Satan's cackle echoed through the chamber.

"There will be no failure, for beasts of boiling blood shall join in army to char the earth about them until all but the woman lie dead and she will be mine."

Herod's faced ripened in a satisfied grin.

"Which demons shall rain down upon them?"

"Demons yes, most foul, which make their way hither to them as we speak," Satan said. "But even more, more, an army sent forth beyond those who traverse the netherworlds to them, an army of pestilence upon the earth that shall both deliver the means to our victory and continue as an iron fist upon the planet as we rule it."

"And from whence shall this army hail?" Herod said.

Satan's eyes bored into the king, and the demon emitted a hollow laugh.

The trumpets sounded and the massive doors of Herod's palace parted.

"The sire of your blood, and the womb of the succubus in which your seed grew," Satan hissed, "shall be their doom."

And through the doors of the palace, into Herod's chamber, strode his son, clad in armor of black and blood.

Herodius.

Half man, half demon, he was an earthquake heaving, colossal, fiery and destructive. His mouth bellowed like a volcano, his nose was sharp and daggered, his eyes were thick and empty like the hollow orbs of a shark, mouth deep in prey. His mien was one of unceasing arrogance and malevolence. His skin was chalk white and pulled taut around the thick, jagged bones of his face, seeming all the more like a ghostly mask of death when ringed by the flowing, stygian rivers of his oily mane.

His armor was slick and slimy, the color of a centipede's skin, spiked with thin nails like the tail of a wasp. On the larger spikes of his arm and abdomen were still decaying chunks of blood and flesh, dried and reeking, from which he would sup, the meat perfuming his breath in the souls of men long gone, the liquid caking his lips and teeth.

He turned to Herod, who smirked to cloak chagrin at his son's appearance.

"My father."

He turned to Satan.

"My Lord."

He lightly bowed, sarcastically, toward each.

"I have returned, to do your bidding."

Herodius summoned forth three of his soldiers, who pulled with them a long chain of mangled corpses.

"And I have brought forth the spoils of my journey," Herodius said, sardonically.

The demon spawn skulked to the string of bones and bodies and pulled one half-eaten head up limply in his claws, turning its bloody stalk to the throne.

"Say hello to your father," Herodius smirked, and his howl filled the room.

THIRTY-THREE

The two Magi strained mightily to keep the portal alive and secure, one to hold it open, the other to throw up barriers when something unearthly and diabolical passed its way, caught the scent of human flesh and souls and, lustful and hungry, tried to shove its way through the gate into the realm of men.

The warriors stood stoic, arms held aloft, sweating and trembling, exhausted. Joseph and Mary watched and sought shelter from the onslaught as the heavens above gathered in gloom and an ever-growing array of ravens hovered overhead, cross-hatching the sky like stitches.

A lightning strike burned to the ground just beyond them, charring a smoking crater. Gaspar called out in pain, falling to his knees, and Melchior was forcefully thrown to the dirt. The gate shrunk quickly, quickly, before being saved by Melchior's outstretched hand. Then it halted, and expanded, barely, barely, as the Magi rose to his feet again, defiant.

The enchanted doorway flickered and sparked, threatened to become nothing but a halo of smoke drifting into embers. But the Magi grew stronger, the amulets around their chest shone brightly through the gathering mist. The gate began to burn and fire and blaze until it grew as a flame gulping at air and engulfing all around it, until it rose to the height of a man and began to burn green and gold again, to glow and vibrate.

And as it widened, Melchior and Gaspar could make out a number of figures, vague and murky, just beyond its opaque face.

They were huge and spiked and horned, inhuman, of horrible countenance, even in shadow. There were a half dozen, maybe more.

But among them were two.

Two.

That looked vaguely human.

Gaspar clenched his fists and steeled himself, maintaining the sacred shield, as he felt buffeted by forces unseen, pummeling him and the air and earth around him.

Melchior remained stoic, solid and rigid as marble, hands raised, endlessly repeating a prayer and blessing from time immemorial, straining to keep the gate alive.

Through the growing light, the pulsating portal, they could see the teeming throng. Dozens, faceless, yet grotesque in shape and form, behind the milky white wall, struggling to get through.

And then they saw two crosses of crimson, emblazoned against the smooth barrier, and, with a burst of white lightning and indigo blue light, two blackened figures hurtled through, glowing bright then dissipating into steam, before turning solid, two human shapes tumbling to the ground.

Balthazar and the Arimathean.

The Arimathean dropped hard, unconscious. Balthazar dragged down with him, but Balthazar quickly regained his composure, just as the first army of pale, spider-veined, oozing arms and tentacles began to poke through the firmament of the portal.

"By the word of God!" he yelled towards the enchanted gate. "Be sealed!"

He raised his arms along with Melchior, chanting in guttural tones, their eyes glowing white, their faces carved in eerie masks, as the portal squeezed slowly smaller, smaller, smaller. Then it lofted into the sky, screaming into the heavens, trailing lightning and sparks behind it as it sealed, hurtling the encroaching hell beasts back to the nether dimensions from whence they sought to escape.

Balthazar fell to his knees, his hands falling hard against the ground, as he breathed laboriously. His robes were cut and burned at odd angles, his body tattered in scars.

Gaspar and Melchior looked at the two men, at the gruesome sight of their rendered flesh.

Irregular and insane gashes and bites covered their forms, particularly about the groin and heart. Some wounds were like those of a lion, others circular and bloody like the jaws of a leech.

And still others were unlike any they had seen on the earth or any nether realm.

Strange oblong rips where their insides seemed to have been partially sucked through the holes.

Others that appeared to have burst their flesh with a series of hooks.

And still others that alternated deep punctures with what appeared to be burns, the skin wrinkled and gray, folded and sagging, and, most disturbingly, seeping a thick, light green pus-like substance.

A perverse part of them churned with macabre curiosity over the wounds, and what the men had endured, but propriety and respect kept them from asking, kept them from doing anything but wincing and trying to staunch the nightmarish chills gathered from each deep, disgusting gash they saw upon their friends.

Melchior acted with haste, scattering healing dusts and oils and whispering prayers to generate a halo of renewing fire about the two men, burning a cool blue, lightly about them, enfolding and embracing them, caressing them. The fire burned until the wounds slowly closed and mended, the pus and slime spewed and dissipated, and, disgustingly, an army of skittering cockroaches and squirming maggots came rampaging out of their mouths, burning in the holy fire and disintegrating, as the two men's bodies became whole and unscathed again.

The Arimathean laid on the ground, and his breath, first deathly, grew in strength, until he coughed and hacked and then, drawing a great gulp of air into his lungs, he lunged forward, lifting up on his feet, glancing about, his eyes shimmering silver and gold, and then, back, back, they turned to burned sienna and charred earth.

He seemed eerily energized, strangely reborn, and, oddly, calm.

He looked around, at Joseph and Mary, then to Gaspar and Melchior, and then, finally, to Balthazar, who was likewise finding his breath.

Their eyes met.

But neither said a word.

And then Balthazar rose to his feet, Melchior helping him up, and looked into the skies, an ashen overcast gray. To the darkened clouds, the ravens nowhere to be found, and the faint outline, drifting and dying, stray sparks where the glowing green portal between worlds once stood.

And, involuntarily, Balthazar's body shook, spasmed in a brief chill, before he caught himself, steeled himself.

"You are back, my friend, and alive," Melchior said. "Your faith has been proven."

But Balthazar's eyes were distant, still staring at the fading gate, far, far from where his body stood, safely away from the haunted remnants still skulking about his mind.

THIRTY-FOUR

Neither Balthazar nor the Arimathean spoke more than a few words on the road to Bethlehem. Both tended to their lingering scars in silence, and neither the other two Magi nor Joseph and Mary pried.

There were countless myths and legends about the paths between worlds, none of them good. All splattered with tales of demons and soul-suckers and succubae attempting to stab their claws into any human, mage or otherwise, who dared to traverse that thorny pathway.

There was distraction enough from the unspoken trek to avoid such talk of their horrors beyond the gate.

"Do you think she'll be able to make it?" Gaspar said quietly to Melchior, both looking at Mary, visibly exhausted and strained.

"I do not know," Melchior said. "We may not make it to Bethlehem proper."

"Fortunately, we need not do so," Balthazar added. "At least not tonight."

Melchior looked at him.

Balthazar nodded.

"I have foreseen it. Outside of town, near the mountainside, where the white dove cages with the dark," Balthazar said, "we will find safe haven."

Just before dusk, as the group made its way through the fields, past figures in the distance, oddly familiar, tending their sheep, they came upon an outcropping of rock adorned with a nearly imperceptible symbol carved lightly into the stone. Balthazar motioned and waved them around it and soon they were upon a humble dwelling.

And just inside its window, a cage, one in which a striking white owl resided.

Seraphim.

Once the men were through the threshold they were greeted warmly by a man and boy.

Simon.

And his father, James.

"I do not say this often of anyone," the Arimathean said, with a slight smile to the boy, "but it is good to see you again."

"We regret to hear of your loss," Balthazar said. "Your father was a good man."

"Thank you," James said.

"And how are your wife, Sarah, and the boy, Jude?" Balthazar said.

"My wife is recovering, slowly," James said. "Very slowly."

"Perhaps we may be of help in that regard," Melchior said.

He motioned to Simon, who returned his salutation and, with Melchior, adjourned to help the woman.

"The boy, remarkably, is fine," James said. "Both boys. Simon was gripped by night terrors but has recovered to where they have passed, or at least lessened in intensity. As for Jude, he sleeps, and dreams with the bliss of the oblivious. I thank God he was spared. That both of them were."

"Their books remain unwritten," Balthazar said.

James nodded.

"You know why we have come," Balthazar said. "The heavens are not yet aligned, and we require sanctuary on passage to Bethlehem, discreet and apart from any eyes prying or, familiar."

"I understand," James said.

James called Simon and asked him to remain guardian at the main entrance, his sword at his belt, his face steely, as James led the group of travelers through a secret door and down into an underground corridor and shelter.

"These rooms should prove comfortable and secure," James said.

Balthazar smiled and thanked him with a nod.

Exhausted, Mary laid down as Joseph made her comfortable, placing a blanket over her and holding her hand while slowly stroking her hair and speaking sotto voce to her. She whispered to him and he nodded, and left the room, walking past the Arimathean, standing sentinel, offering a greeting.

She looked towards the man hovering in the doorway and smiled softly at him.

"How are you holding up?" The Arimathean said.

"Much better than we would be without you, and your friends."

With a humble nod acknowledging her gratitude, the Arimathean looked down, away from her.

Mary exhaled with a small laugh.

The Arimathean glanced back at her.

"You wonder how I can continue on, how I can maintain my faith, my happiness, when death and darkness looms to engulf us," she said.

He began to speak, but halted.

"I understand," she said. "It has been, difficult, of course. Our faith is pure, but we are human, we have fears and doubts, like any others."

The Arimathean nodded slightly.

"But how is this moment different than any other?" she said. "None of us know the time or means of our demise, ever. So why worry of it?"

"I am... not," the Arimathean began.

"We have but one choice between birth and death, and that is how to live our life," she said. "In faith and happiness, or in doubt and fear. You may, or may not, believe in a life beyond this one, but that decision is separate from it. And that simple choice will make all the difference in the path leading to it."

The Arimathean gazed upon her and smiled slightly.

"I have faith in God, yes," Mary said. "But I also have faith in those He has sent to protect us."

She looked into his eyes, and smiled.

"I have faith in you. And so does He."

The Arimathean kept her gaze, contemplating, then turned away, as Joseph returned, bearing a tray with a bowl of soup and a cup of water for his wife.

"Thank you for watching over her," Joseph said to the Arimathean.

The Arimathean nodded, turning to leave, but, for just a moment, he paused, paused, to watch the man with his wife, and for a moment, he remembered. He remembered. His own wife. His own child. Him. A man, a different man, so long ago. A moment that seemed so far removed, yet not so far, at all.

His eyes cloudy, he walked to the Magi waiting in the next room.

Gaspar, with barely a nod to Balthazar, moved to the door by the couple's room, standing guard. Balthazar and the Arimathean walked upstairs, and out the door, to remain on watch as Melchior continued to tend to the ailing wife of James, who laid in the room with the sleeping Jude, never wanting to be more than a few feet from him at any time.

James and Simon brought Balthazar and the Arimathean food and drink, and engaged them in light conversation, before James sent the boy to bed, and then, James adjourned as well.

Balthazar and the Arimathean sat silent, watching the skies.

The Arimathean looked at the serene silhouette of the Magi, dark and tawny, a leopard in repose. He gazed at Balthazar's tattered robes, the Magi's wounds already miraculously healed, his scars almost completely faded, as the Magi sat quietly, eyeing the skies, remarkably serene.

The Arimathean looked away, at the ground, then to the heavens, and back to Balthazar again.

"Thank you."

A slight smile appeared on Balthazar's face.

"There is no need," Balthazar said.

"There is," the Arimathean said.

Balthazar looked at his friend, with a knowing smile.

"As a wise man once said to me, we each have but one life," Balthazar said. "And no greater honor given than to sacrifice it for another."

Balthazar looked into the horizon, as the Arimathean's golden burned sienna eyes remained upon him.

"And as I recall," Balthazar said. "You once did the same for me, as well."

THIRTY-FIVE

Within Herod's temple, flames rose as servants screamed in pain and begged for pity before being molested and slain.

As the stinking bowels before the throne rose in spines of new dead, black flames licked the air and a frenzy whipped among an army of demons that emerged, thrashing and bloody, from the coal dark pit of death that had once almost held certain doom for the Magi.

With a new six-hundred-and-sixty-six ritually slain, their blood drained into the maw, it crackled with fire as Herod and Satan cackled at the hideous beasts to emerge from its murky depths of sorcery, to join in formation with Herodius' vile and lecherous troops.

When the innards of the hole had been drained and cracked dry, the fear-saturated blood now flowing through the horrible demon flesh arrayed before them, Herod and Satan gazed lustily upon their throng, and then out the arched windows at the sky, black with lightning, at an oozing portal coming to life.

The last beast to emerge from the sacrificial pit was the most powerful, a higher demon, in full battle regalia, who scowled at Herod upon his throne and kneeled before Satan, awaiting orders.

Herodius stepped beside it, and likewise genuflected, at both throne and devil.

Satan and Herod grinned with gleeful malice.

"How dare you presume to lead an army of unholy," the demon growled to Herodius.

"More than presume, I assume the mantle without question, and you shall follow, in life or death, as sup for Cerberus," Herodius said.

"You half-blood weakling human scum of a succubus' loins," the demon spat, drawing his sword as the two erupted in battle, to the drooling cheers and stomps of the demonic pack before them.

"It appears we have a bit of a sibling rivalry," Herod said.

He raised his bejeweled goblet and snapped his fingers and a servant appeared, filling it with a mix of blood, wine and occult spices.

Herod took a long drink and smiled as the two warriors circled each other.

They viciously locked steel and arms and Herodius drew the demon in tight against him, slashing his forearm against the hell-spawn's face, the spikes of his armor ripping the crimson flesh of the demon and sending a spurt of burning acidic blood across the demon's eyes, blinding it momentarily, causing the seed of Hades to jerk its head back, exposing its neck to Herodius.

The son of Herod and hell spawn wasted little time, his chiseled fangs tearing into the jugular of the soulless beast. He bit down hard, paying no heed to the sizzle of acidic demon blood singeing his flesh, his sinister laugh staunched by the hunks of unholy meat being ripped forth by his mouth. He hurtled his head back like a lion, mouth heavy with meat and spat it out, as his opponent heaved and spasmed and breathed his last.

With the collapsed demon's arms falling limply to its side, Herodius finished the act. His fanged teeth ripped fully through the hell spawn's neck and tore its head from its body. Then Herodius went in for a disgusting denouement, putting his lips to the demon's and emerging with the beast's rent tongue fresh and bloodied in his teeth, soon devoured.

"A tongue all the more delicious when seared of its poisonous words," Herodius said.

He cackled and smirked at Herod and Satan, then lifted his broadsword in one hand and the defeated beast's head in the other, and turned to the army of demons and soulless men gone past the precipice of insanity.

"You follow me! To crush this world in our jaws and drain its blood to the marrow!"

They chanted madly in unison, slathering and frothing in a horrendous animalistic rage, and Herodius kicked the body and threw the head of his vanquished foe to them, and they tore them apart, devouring them raw before him.

Herodius approached the throne.

"Your will, my lords?"

Satan's eyes glared saturnine and savage. He hissed a forked tongue at the blood-bathed warrior.

"You know what to do. Our beasts stalk them as we speak. By the time you arrive they may be nothing but meat for flies. You may feast and sate your loins on what remains. But the woman and her unborn are mine. They will return untouched and unmolested, confined to the Cage of Domitae, the prison between worlds, which hies to them on fanged wings and clawed back. Should you fail my orders your soul will pay for all eternity."

Herodius smirked.

"The will of the true lord be done."

THIRTY-SIX

Dawn arched over the earth as the bedraggled travelers returned to the road. As the night cusped into day they could see the last vestiges of the holy path in the sky, the stars aligned just below the moon, now almost completely in a straight line, pointing into the horizon directly in front of them, then disappearing, eclipsed by the light of a new day.

They moved briskly through the hours, always on guard. By early evening they had Bethlehem proper within their sights, the farms and fields of the small city stretching out before them to welcome them into its bosom.

"We are almost there," Joseph said to Mary, reassuringly, kissing her forehead.

"Tonight the stars align, and all shall be protected," Melchior said.

"But still, these last hours of the day remain," Gaspar said.

"This seems too easy," the Arimathean said, looking ahead. "There is no way they let us into that city without a fight."

"You had to say it, didn't you?" Gaspar said, sighing and looking back at the wicked sliver that had begun to materialize in the sky as the sun set.

Behind them, floating in the distance, through the setting sun, they saw a strange light, eerie green, a slit against the fading orange orb, a reptilian eye.

The occult illuminant crackled and fizzled and descended at a sloth's pace from the sky in a hail of wretched yellow pus and viscous ochre slime.

"I had to open my big mouth," the Arimathean said.

Melchior nodded to Balthazar who likewise noted the passage of the rift in the heavens.

"The gateway between worlds," Melchior said. "We thought it closed."

"It was," Balthazar said.

"But once closed, it would take an incredible amount of power to open it once more, particularly within the same moon cycle," Melchior said.

"Obviously something else wished it to open once more," Balthazar said.

"But who would have the power to…"

They looked at each other with trepidation.

"Satan."

"Did you not say that whatever comes through it can return the same way?" Gaspar said. "Perhaps our magicks are enough to send these forthcoming visitors back to whence they came?"

"Our occult materials are scarce, nowhere near enough to re-open it and send them back," Melchior said. "We have no choice but battle."

"When have we had another?" the Arimathean said.

Balthazar scanned the horizon. "For now, though, in the few moments we have, we must flee, to find shelter if we can, for the man and woman."

They spurred their horses and Joseph and Mary joined alongside, furiously stomping across the soft farm ground toward Bethlehem, seeking refuge, shelter, any means of finding safety until the welcome blanket of the night sky could arrive, the heavenly alignment bringing them safe haven, or an ironic coda to a violent end.

Just inside the outskirts of the city, they saw a series of farms and humble dwellings, shacks and mangers, used by the shepherds to keep their sheep and find solace during storms. As they approached one upon a grassy hill, the sky grew gray about them, and the green lightning and burning hail began to fall, and the Magi, Arimathean and Joseph and Mary hurtled over a hill and drew their horses to halt in the humble embrace of a simple shack, raw boards smacked together over hay, where the animals had begun to gather in fear of the crackling skies.

"What, is there no room at the inn?" the Arimathean said, as they huddled within the ramshackle shelter.

"We have no choice, we need to stop here," Balthazar said, turning to Joseph and Mary, "The storm is too dense to continue. Stay here, and we shall be guardians over you to the death."

"We are in Bethlehem proper, within the sacred spires," Melchior said. "We need only make it to the sunset."

"If only that were as easy as it sounds," the Arimathean said.

The Magi and the Arimathean left the man and woman within, and the warriors strode to the edge of the pathetic dwelling's mouth, awaiting their fate, their potential doom.

The hell portal had stopped and hovered high in the ripped heavens above them. It boiled, bellowing and throbbing, spewing crud and pestilence, spitting fire and lightning throughout the gray skies, and then, with a final heaving that sent a scattering of flame and vomit and an unholy howl through the air, the darkling figures began to emerge from its decrepit maw.

Balthazar trained his eyes upon them.

"The Xyzy'Aryxl'faa," Balthazar said.

"The what?" the Arimathean said.

"Swarms of demons from the lowest depths, with the bodies and claws of lions, the tails and stings of scorpions, the wings of bats and the faces of jackals melded with the visages of demons, five eyes among them and three spewing mouths of forked tongues and acrid frothing bile."

"Sounds like fun."

"They will not kill, at least not immediately, they prefer to toy with their victims, until demolishing and devouring them," Balthazar said. "They will attack the mind and heart, torturing the victim. Their stings carry the power to poison the souls of men and bring forth that which might bring madness and the farthest depths to your soul, which only causes them to swarm and feed all the more on your fury and panic. Once they sense they have saturated the victim's body with enough fear to lower its vibration to make the trip to hell, they kill it and drag its soul down to the depths with it to torture it in eternity."

"So, in other words, psychic attack," the Arimathean said, clutching the Revelator's amulet around his neck.

"Yes," Balthazar said. "As long as the amulets are about us, the demons' stings, fangs and claws, painful as they may be, are their sole weapons, and they may only inflict a human death."

"Only," Gaspar said.

"And if they are emerging from the hellgate," Balthazar said, "they will be followed by the beast that sires them. . ."

"Guilgotha!"

The two other Magi froze, stunned at the sight of the legendary demon.

"The defiler," Melchior said. "Another demon of psychic attack, but whose corpulent ooze surrounds its victim and keeps it alive for one hundred years as it slowly digests it."

"So one distracts and knocks you out so the other can engulf and eat you slowly," the Arimathean said. "Nice."

"Or keeps you alive so that you can be extracted later for more insidious means," Melchior said.

"But," Balthazar said, "that seems odd…"

"What?" Melchior said.

Balthazar paused, contemplating.

"So how do we kill them?" the Arimathean said.

"They feed on doubt, on fear, so the best way to weaken them is to control your feelings, and deny them strength," Melchior said. "Steel will harm them and keep them at bay, but the only way to slay them is by the sacred swords."

"And what is that?" the Arimathean said, pointing to a murky mass emerging from the hellhole with the demons, morphing into a glowing, ornate box of onyx and gold straps arrayed with precious gems and armored with long, thin spikes of shimmering steel at each of its corners.

Balthazar froze.

"Melchior, quickly, by any means! We must attempt to close the gate!"

THIRTY-SEVEN

Balthazar shot his hands heavenward to form an energy shield, attempting to keep the gate at bay.

"Melchior!"

"But, I do not..."

"It is weak while those pass through it! Use all your charms if need be, but it must be closed!"

"I can attempt to, but I cannot say..."

Melchior began to empty his pouches of charms, smashing them to the ground as he hurled incantations into the air, smoke and flame rising about him.

"What is that box?" the Arimathean said.

"Something even more diabolical than I imagined," Balthazar said, his face stunned in recognition, for the device, as well as for what he assumed it was meant to be used in combination with the demons.

"The Cage of Domitae, an infinite limbo, in which a being or soul can be caught forever, and can only be retrieved upon recitation of ancient spells known by none but a few."

"And they are trying to capture us in that?" the Arimathean asked. "Or in Guilgotha?"

"Not us," Balthazar said. "The woman and her child."

"But why, when they have been trying to kill them?" Gaspar asked.

"Herod has been trying to kill them," Balthazar said. "The demons arrayed before us prove Satan is in control now, and he knows full well the power they possess."

Balthazar looked to the couple, then his companions.

"They seek to possess her, fill her with demons, condemn her soul and poison her heart," Balthazar said. "That is why they sent these parasites of the heart and mind! Surely they had seen our battle with the soul rapers through the hellgate and known psychic attack to be useless against us. Our deaths are assumed, an afterthought, overwhelmed by the sheer mass of enemies attacking us. Guilgotha and the Xyzy'Aryxl'faa are meant to taint the woman, to attempt to eclipse and corrupt her so they can abduct her for satanic ritual!"

"For what ritual?" Gaspar said.

"A satanic sacrifice, of the mother, in which they will extract the unborn and attempt to transform him into the darkest of evils, the anti-Christ."

"Can they do that?" Melchior said.

"We dare not risk finding out," Balthazar said.

The Arimathean looked back to Joseph and Mary, the man holding her hand, his arm around her, the woman, now prone on the ground, sweating and red, her eyes pursed in pain.

He ran to them and quickly pulled the amulet from around his neck to put around hers.

"Take it!" he shouted over their protestations, putting it around her neck.

In a flash, Balthazar was beside him, taking off his own amulet, to give to the Arimathean.

The Arimathean refused.

"You must," Balthazar said, looking him in the eye. "I am of greater strength in the arcane arts. And as powerful as the demons you fight on the battlefield are, those within you may be more so."

The Arimathean, reluctantly, threw the amulet around his neck. It hung loose over his robes around his chest.

"Balthazar, we may have another problem here," Gaspar said, nodding to Mary. "She is very near to birth."

Balthazar glanced at her, raised his arms and his eyes began to burn light blue and blinding white and he covered the couple in a cloak of invisibility, just as the first wall of demons rampaged towards them.

Behind the flying beasts was the monster of the depths, Guilgotha the Depraved, an oscillating mass of blood and pus and feces, from which would burst claws, fangs and jagged stings, but also, visions of the most grotesque and cruel punishments.

As Guilgotha approached the field of battle, each of the Magi felt a cracking sound at the base of his neck, an oppressive shove into his psyche for just a moment, before he was able to exorcise it through means of the Revelator's charms and his own will.

But even with the sigils and charms and protections of the Revelator, Guilgotha was too powerful, could not be entirely thwarted. For while it could not burrow into the men's minds through magickal means, to secret away the identities of those they held most dear, it meant to inflict psychological wounds in other ways, displaying among its gelatinous mass disgusting tableaus of the warriors being killed and defiled in the stark fields of hell, tortured and dragged through gardens of thorns and human waste.

"They are only illusions meant to distract!" Balthazar cried. "They are not real!"

But they were real enough to halt the men for a moment.

A lethal moment, which allowed the Xyzy'Aryxl'faa to swarm them, the hell beasts' stings burning the men's flesh with a frenetic tornado of tiny deaths.

THIRTY-EIGHT

The warriors exploded upon their foes with lightning
strikes, blades in both hands, one to kill, one to maim, both in
valiant attempts to ward off the relentless attack of slashes and
punctures pummeling their skin.

Gaspar's girth and mass proved best suited to the attack,
as his powerful thrusts of his weapon not only dispelled
countless sub-demons, but the mighty swaths created by his
strikes sent their wings bent and hurtling from him, stunning
them and allowing him to slay all the more in their paralysis.

Melchior's agility and speed proved resourceful as he
managed to whirl and avoid a plethora of concerted strikes and
even diverted several of the stings to stab into the bodies of the
demons, their weapons proving their own demise.

The Arimathean used his strength and agility to suppress
and expel the attacks, his lightning swordsmanship devastating
the armies of flying doom beset upon him, ripping a jagged

symphony of strikes throughout the air, creating a maze nearly impenetrable by the demon hordes.

Balthazar eschewed his sword as his primary weapon, utilizing his magickal powers to deceive and destroy the demons about him with sacred fire and illusions diverting and distracting them, leading them to their deaths.

But as many as they killed, they seemed to be gaining little or no ground in the battle.

Guilgotha's odorous maw belched a wretched scent as the demon laughed heartily, its obese mass circling the battlefield slowly, insistently.

The crackle of the dead exoskeletons of dozens of Xyzy'Aryxl'faa crumpled in the air as Guilgotha's girth grew closer, closer, over the bodies of his sub-demons killed by the warriors and scattered to the winds.

And as Guilgotha's mass slathered over the corpses, they came to life again, larger and more frantic than before, swarming the warriors in ebon clouds of doom.

The men's swords swirled, decimating their foes, but could not stop the endless waves of creatures. The men's moves grew wild and frenzied as the attackers' venom began to flow, and even with their supernatural constitutions, they began to feel leaden as their veins scalded with the fiery invasion of poison.

With a series of quicksilver swings, the Arimathean destroyed nearly three dozen of the beasts, but his movements were too severe, and the amulet about his neck, already loose, became exposed and flailing, a glowing orb whipping about him on its loping leash.

The demons seized upon it, biting through the chain and pulling it from him, and instantly, there was a crack of lightning that charred the ground, as the demons felt his passion, his anger, and knew, knew he was vulnerable.

Guilgotha's deep, murky laugh filled the air, and suddenly, the Arimathean felt as if the base of his skull shattered within his head, felt as if a basket of cobras whirled throughout his brain.

Guilgotha rose up above the battle, hovering over the Arimathean and amidst the broken teeth and nails extruding from its virulent mass, were dismembered torsos and heads without bodies which would wallow through the disgusting murk long enough to cry out in pain and bury tears of sorrow.

When the sobbing was heard from the dismembered bodies churning within Guilgotha's mass, it made the hair on the Arimathean's neck stand at end.

For the faces choking in the waste of the demon's body, the visages were those of his loved ones, dead and gone.

His wife.

His children.

Now pale, gagging, sobbing, begging for mercy within the monster's fetid flesh.

Distracting the Arimathean, driving him slowly to madness, as the swarming demons' onslaught grew more fiery and virulent, the stings increasing, increasing, as the venom began to burn, ever more, like his anger, through his veins.

THIRTY-NINE

"Father! Father! Please help us! It hurts! It hurts! Help me father! The pain! It's hurting me so much! Please! Please!"

The Arimathean trembled with a combination of sorrow, fear and hatred as he struggled to keep his bearings, continuing to swing his sword against the thickening mass of winged demons mobbing him.

"No! No! Not again! Please! Please!" the weeping voice of his wife shrieked as a horrifying tableaux of debasement played out just beneath the bulbous flesh of Golgotha. "Help me! Help me! No!"

Tears began to flow from the Arimathean's eyes, down his ruddy, leathered face as he attempted to battle on, but even without looking toward Guilgotha, the images splattered repeatedly through his head, unimaginable tortures and perverse defilings of the ones he held dearest.

"Do not pay it heed!" Melchior called out, sensing the Arimathean's plight even as he battled for his own life. "They are not the souls you hold most dear, who dwell in heaven; these are but the foul illusions, trickery to cut to the quick of your heart! The more you doubt, the more you fear, the more you allow them to manifest the power to slay you!"

But still, the Arimathean boiled, transfixed by the sights in his brain, and as he did, he seethed in anger and sadness and was blanketed all the more by the lesser demons, sinking their venom into his flesh.

With a berserker howl, he flailed his sword about him, tearing them out of the air to explode and splatter in a hail of sparks and flame and putrid white and sickly yellow globs upon the ground that sizzled and emitted a decrepit stench. But as his rage blossomed and bled, the demons multiplied, and Guilgotha's disgusting deceptions reeked ever more perverted in the Arimathean's mind.

The other Magi could do little more than he, furiously whipping their weapons about to combat the swarm, unable to unleash any magicks to shield themselves.

Except for Balthazar.

The great wizard's mind raced, his prayers and incantations at the ready, sacred herbs and talismans flung to the ground before him hastily, like transcendental land mines, awaiting activation.

As with the others, the demons had swarmed him, but unlike his companions, his stoicism and calm kept their attacks from seething with the power inflicted upon the others. Given a wider berth, Balthazar managed to thwart them by throwing up a cloak of fire and mist. Beneath it, he conjured a holographic image of himself battling, which revealed itself to the flying demons once the mist subsided, causing them to rain upon the illusion. While the beasts were thus distracted, Balthazar was able to slip back into the meager spot where Joseph and Mary took shelter.

He cloaked himself in invisibility like the couple, but it could not last more than a few moments, enough for him to gain a perspective on the battle, as the swarms slowly, bit by bit, claimed the flesh of his fellow warriors.

For every demon slain, another three took its place out of the hemorrhaging maw of Guilgotha, and quickly enough, the oozing mass of the elder demon was upon them as well. His obese muck raining the decaying remains of souls decimated in the outer realms of hell upon them, each blackened web of waste attaching and burning through their skin until they sloughed it aside.

But even more disturbing was how the elder demon grew larger and larger, feeding upon the emotion of the battle. And as its girth expanded, it drew a circle tightening about them, a tide of slime and nightmare images of death and depravity growing, growing, and rising above them, and the shelter of Joseph and Mary.

Balthazar noticed his holograph begin to disintegrate, and the swarms about it begin to seek new prey, to seek him.

And in the midst of it all, hovering, was the gaping maw of the Cage of Domitae, singing its hymn, seeking souls.

Seeking one soul in particular.

In a burst, it was upon them, the cage at last thrusting through the illusion of invisibility with a mind of its own, a demon sentience, knowing, seeking, the souls which it was sent to steal.

The mother and unborn which it was sent to enslave.

Its maw became agape and a hurricane wind whipped forth to suck in its prey.

But Balthazar was prepared.

The mage stood at the side of Joseph and Mary and began to utter prayers loud and constant as fire burst from his hands. He thrust his long fingers into a leather pouch at his waist and began throwing handfuls of sacred myrrh about the heavens, the golden powder of death and new life transcendent haloing the space about them in a shower of blue flame. It halted the Cage of Domitae and sent it spinning in rapid circles barely the length of a man above them, unable to escape the whirlpool.

Balthazar raised his holy sword and carved a runed pattern in the air and the shimmering sigil hovered, hanging in a mist. The fiery symbol swirled and coagulated into a titanic set of wings, iridescent and inescapable, which wrapped around the battlefield and froze the demons and Guilgotha in their tracks, crystalizing them and shattering them into countless pieces which were then swept through the skies and into the gaping maw of the Cage of Domitae.

In a frenzied tornado of flame and fury, they were sucked into its portal and with a mighty wave of his hand, Balthazar closed the door and sealed the Cage shut. The box's spikes withdrew into its sides and it dropped to the ground, smoking, seething and glowing like a candle flame occluded.

The warriors collapsed to the ground, relieved, in pain and exhaustion.

The sun began to fade, shallow, upon the horizon, the first stars and the outlines of the moon began to come into view beyond the watercolor pale blue of the day seeping into night.

Gaspar, Melchior and the Arimathean laid upon the earth, panting, sweating, as Balthazar strode among them, chanting a healing spell, as a blue-silver glow began to rise from his hands and hover above them, revitalizing them as they rose to their feet.

Just in time to feel the ground beneath them shudder.

"What is that?"

They heard the battle cries first, echoing across the dirt as the advancing army stomped out a dismal dirge, barreling relentlessly towards them.

A tremendous swath of demons, a disease spreading across the land.

And at the fore, leading them, a giant in ebon armor that shined like the skin of a snake.

"Is that?" Gaspar said.

"Herodius," the Arimathean said, through gritted teeth.

FORTY

The Arimathean's sword flew to his hand by instinct, his mighty fingers clasped tight around it, as his blood boiled and his heart thundered within his chest.

"Herodius," Melchior said, fixed on the horde rampaging over the horizon. "There is no doubt."

"The son of Herod and a demon's womb," Gaspar said, "and about a hundred other demons, as well, from the looks of it."

"He is only one man, one battle, not the war," Melchior said to the Arimathean. "We must remain focused; surround the manger of the man and woman on all sides, be wary of the horde in total. This is Satan's last grasp at victory before nightfall, no doubt it will be the most furious and desperate."

"Is there room for them in the Cage of Domitae?" Gaspar said. "They would appear good company for its current inhabitants."

"I sense traditional magicks will not work against them, not on a grand scale, to allow us to send them into the void like the others," Balthazar said. "They are under the full of Satan's claw, and all the more, tethered to the earth in sorcery and thereby immune to such sweeping banishment."

"Then we will dispatch them in a more traditional way," Gaspar said, drawing his holy sword.

The remaining three clasped their sacred blades as well, readying themselves, backs against the walls of the manger, seconds away from battle, when they heard the first cry.

Then another.

From behind them.

From within.

The Arimathean and Gaspar looked at one another, then to Melchior, as Joseph cried out to them.

"It's Mary! She is in labor! The child is on its way!"

Beyond them, closer and closer, louder and louder, they heard the demons' growls and wails scream nearer.

The Arimathean, Gaspar and Melchior advanced from the manger to meet the oncoming horde, but Balthazar remained behind, his attention distracted, divided between preparing enchantments of safety for the man and woman, and girding against the onslaught.

His back was turned to the oncoming fray, his arms stretched in completion of a shield of protection and power around the couple. It had just materialized when he was caught unaware, as a seething frenzy of black adders soared through the air towards the shack, enchanted arrows from the unholy archers bounding over the hill.

Balthazar's precognition and reflexes enabled him to throw his cape around himself and the couple and cast a spell to dissipate most, but not all, of the biting shanks. He managed to protect the two, but not himself, as more than a dozen pierced his flesh and sent him to the ground in agony.

"Poisoned…" he gasped.

His consciousness fading, he looked up to see an ocean of flying death above him, more arrows of the damned sent sailing towards him and the couple. But as he struggled to remain conscious, he sent a desperate plea, a prayer of blinding light into the heavens, into the arms of the gathering night.

Immediately around him he felt a halo of power and protection wash over him and the couple, he felt the arrows sailing towards them as well as those already stabbing him dissolve and waft away as smoke. He saw the white and silver figure who had haunted his dreams, the warrior enchantress, standing above them, and with a wave of her arms, all arrows sent their way froze and melted to ash and mist, sailing impotently adrift in a soft breeze.

Balthazar felt a rush of wind as he looked up, into her face, their violet eyes meeting, and a slight smile on her face, before she disappeared.

The unholy army was about to pounce upon them when the Arimathean, his faced pursed, turned to Balthazar.

"Wait! Why would they send their archers firing towards the woman when it seemed the demons and the cage were arrayed to capture her?"

But his question went unanswered as the first of the rabid army of hellions smashed into them, weapons clashing, teeth thrashing, as they erupted in battle.

Mere minutes remained until night.

Minutes to death, or the promise of life.

FORTY-ONE

The initial surge of the demon army blitzed them feverishly, jagged toothed blades sizzling through the air, ringing the sound of holy steel upon the unholy teeth of Satan's army across the fields of Bethlehem.

Gaspar, Melchior and the Arimathean had closed ranks in front of the wounded Balthazar and Joseph and Mary, the woman crying out, her child straining to enter the world as the last rays of the sun disappeared into the distance, the holy stars alight and aligning above them, the energy fields of the earth comingling with the coming night, causing the ground to curdle and grumble.

The mass of demons frenetically stormed the outnumbered warriors, but still, battling with all of their might and guile, they managed to hold them off, barely, barely.

However, in the chaos, a cunning viper slithered stealthily through the distracted warriors' ranks.

The darkling Herodius, sword at the ready, strode through the throes of battle, to the whirling, spinning box of the Cage of Domitae, now recovered and hovering above the field of horror, and commanded it forward.

Balthazar tumbled on the last thread of consciousness, and as he felt himself drift, he heard a voice, was buffeted by a light, and saw again, the woman in white and silver, the angel, the sentinel of his dreams, aloft before his eyes, her mouth open, uttering words soft and enchanting, revitalizing, hopeful.

He felt a surge through him, and found the vigor to reach into his cloak and pull forth a small ivory horn, which he had been given, as a gift, a reminder, a tribute of gratitude, for lives saved, once lost, now found once more.

Seeing the demon sea cresting upon the warriors, his beloved friends, he blew into the horn, with his last remaining strength. Its cry was heard across the land, a tremendous call of unearthly beauty that caused the demons and Herodius to halt in pain and allowed the Magi to slash their way through those immediately about them, their bodies piling up and kicked aside.

As the bellow of the beacon echoed about the lands, the ground beyond the demons began to quake all the more, and across the hill, teeming upon the horizon, came an army of shepherds, swords and axes at the ready, to do battle with the frothing demon plague.

Facing a new attack from behind as well, the demons became confused and divided, allowing Melchior the ability to cast spells of flame and fury, to dispatch great swaths of the enemy. Gaspar's axe and sword sent almost equal numbers back to the hell from whence they came and the Arimathean's swords tore through them and painted the ground with their horrible blood.

With his remaining breaths of vitality spent, Balthazar collapsed to the ground, the unearthly poison of the arrows teeming through his veins, encircling his heart as his waning magicks prevented it from penetrating the core of his being and dragging him to the grave.

However, the last thing he saw as he faded from consciousness was the last he ever wished to see.

The shadow of a hulking evil, having somehow made its way through their lines in the thick of battle, to the heart of their camp, to the very side of those they had pledged their lives to protect.

A figure that cleaved the curtain of chaos, knifed through the demons and strife, hurled away Balthazar's limp body and made his way to the woman about to give birth to the child they had traversed hell and earth to protect.

Whether the demon-spawn meant to capture or to kill her, Balthazar could not know as he valiantly struggled, but failed, to retain consciousness.

He could only dread.

As his last sight was of a horrific monster towering over them.

Herodius.

Looming above Herod's half-son, the Cage of Domitae hung, trailing him, before slithering down towards the man and the woman, its gaping maw opening up to pull her and the half-born child in, as Herodius' sword raised above Joseph and Mary.

She laid in the hay, helpless, in the throes of labor as Joseph threw his body over hers to shield her.

Herodius' enchanted rune sword swung down.

And shattered the cage to bits.

Herodius laughed deeply, and his gaze slathered lustily upon Mary.

"How dare your spawn presume to rule upon my throne?" Herodius spat. "How dare yet another satanic brother be brought forth to combat me for that which is rightfully mine, my father's heart and crown?"

Herodius scowled over the woman.

"I thought of killing you, raining poison down upon you all, and devouring your flesh as I ripped the unborn from your insides for my own spells of transformation and demonization," Herodius said. "However, that was not to be, and so be it. I find it more pleasing to keep you alive. With all heaven, hell and earth mine to rule, with you as my bride and the anti-Christ as our son, enslaved to me, I shall not only usurp and destroy my father, but even Satan shall bow to us!"

He lunged towards Joseph and Mary, tossing Joseph aside as he rose to defend his wife, and reaching a thick, black claw to grab Mary's arm.

But before Herodius could defile her with even the slightest touch, the slash of a sacred blade rang through the air between them. Herodius' half-demon reflexes were all that saved him from death, as he sailed backwards, throwing his own accursed rune blade up in defense as he was driven back, thrown to the ground by the force of the blow.

Herodius was stunned for an instant, but collected himself, and rose with a sardonic smile, a wicked chuckle.

Standing tall, bloodied but unbowed, between Herodius and the couple, was the Arimathean, his teeth clenched, his brow astorm, swords drawn, as he scowled at the face of the man he had sworn to kill.

The Arimathean's charred earth eyes met the fiery hell pits of Herodius' orbs and he spat on the ground between them, growling.

"Not this time."

FORTY-TWO

With a diabolical cackle, Herodius drew his second weapon and dual blood-red rune swords that sparked of Saturnian fire furied upon the Arimathean, who dug in hard to deflect the attack, parrying with his own two blades.

The Arimathean battled feverishly. In one hand, he clasped the holy sword of S'iam B'ala. In the other, his well-worn steel that dripped of hundreds of lives taken, demon and man. He remained steadfast, fending off Herodius' twin-fanged assault.

The half-demon's blades thundered down upon the Arimathean but every attack was met with equal ferocity, the human's swords slashing and exploding against the accursed weapons of hades spiking from Herodius' massive fists.

As the night fell, the Magi and shepherds clashed with the remaining demons among the quaking earth. Glowing green lightning tore the skies asunder and deafening thunder roared across the lands. And within the ramshackle shed, mere feet away from the woman moments from birth, the Arimathean and Herodius hurtled at each other, curses scalding the air, swords colliding in a diabolical orgy of hate, neither giving way.

In the midst of the battle, despite his wounds, the Arimathean grew increasingly stronger, stronger, as he felt himself filled with an energy he had never before encountered. However, it was beyond vengeance, beyond hatred, beyond the righteousness he had held so deep inside his heart to mete upon the unclean soul of his darkest enemy, the one who'd taken all away from him.

He felt a power far beyond, one he couldn't explain, but one which kept him always at the attack, always one step ahead, always on the aggressive, against a foe of half-demon, half-human blood who had slain and devoured men of far greater stature than he.

However, in the last seconds of the day, the Arimathean seemed to recognize this and question his strength, to feel the slightest twinge of doubt in his abilities.

As if sensing the Arimathean's hesitation, Herodius pounced upon him, thrusting through his defenses and barely missing a death blow, blocked by the Arimathean. But still, the force of which knocked the human aside, down to the ground, into the dirt and hay, stunned for just a moment.

Herodius stopped himself from lunging at the downed foe, noticed the sun at a sliver and knew his time was short. He lifted his blades to deal a killing strike to the woman, seeking to decapitate her, as she screamed out in fear and pain.

"If you shall not take my hand, you shall die by it, and I will rip my slave scion from your fading womb!"

But as the stars aligned in the sky and the night emerged in full, the Arimathean burst from the ground, alight and burning for vengeance. His eyes astorm, his swords slicing through the air towards his hated foe, he blocked the lethal swath intended for Mary and knocked Herodius back on his knees.

The Arimathean took no mercy, heaving his steel down upon his stunned nemesis. Herodius turned just in time to parry the herculean attack, and rise to his feet, but the Arimathean would not be halted. There was no doubt within him now, no hesitation.

The Arimathean was relentless, upon Herodius like a wild animal, savage and untamed, his blades erupting through the air, shoving Herodius back, back, away from the sacred birth, until, at last gasp, the Arimathean pummeled him to the ground, the sardonic smirk so long upon Herodius' lips now little but a shocked, frightened grimace.

The Arimathean continued to thrash away, his body suddenly alight with a magickal energy, unstoppable, unquenchable. Herodius fell before him, bleeding and gored, as with a last mighty blow, the Arimathean smashed Herodius' swords from him, sending them soaring into the night.

The leader of the unholy army lay defeated on the dirt, spent and breathing heavily, his armor frayed and broken, carved and sliced and dripping blackened blood. The son of Herod, fallen before his conqueror.

A revenge finally quenched.

The Arimathean looked into the eyes of the half-demon, half-man and saw something he had never seen before within him, or anyone like him.

Fear.

For a moment, the Arimathean stopped, his sword arms fallen by his side, a calm over his body.

As the night blanketed the earth in full and the stars aligned, the ground started to quake mightily and Herodius slumped away, crawling, backing from the battle in retreat, gravely wounded.

The Arimathean looked into the black void eyes of his vanquished, gazed into the sad, pathetic, empty realms within Herodius, and as the stars emblazoned above them he no longer felt a need for vengeance, no longer felt a burning through his soul, and instead, felt an unfamiliar peace, a victory of his own.

The Arimathean turned to Joseph and Mary, turned to the baby being born, to the sound of the infant's cries, the sight of the mother's tears through a smile, as her husband held his arm around her and kissed her cheek, a tear of joy curving down his face.

For a moment, the Arimathean allowed himself a moment of happiness.

Then, over his shoulder, he felt the pall of pure evil once more looming.

He turned to see the jagged teeth of Herodius' broken rune swords hurling towards him, towards the woman and child. It was a potentially decimating blow, but the Arimathean was too fast, too quick, and his aim was true, his swords pure.

With one mighty swath of the sacred blade, the Arimathean severed Herodius' arms at the wrists, the claws and swords dropping harmless to the dirt before him. And with a second deadly arc of his broadsword, the Arimathean sent Herodius' head, frozen in terror, hurtling away from its torso. It arched down a hill, into the distance, and flew into flame, disintegrating into nothingness.

Dealing a tremendous kick to the headless mass before him, the Arimathean exploded the last of Herodius the Wicked into the maw of darkness beyond, as each remnant of him burned into blackened coal, his soul fouled to hell, before the ashes of his body's remains even touched the ground.

The night fallen, the heavens in alignment, the child born and upon the earth, the demons were unable to hold their growingly tenuous grasp upon the earthen dimension. With wild shrieks and writhing, they burst into flame and dissipated, howling, into the ether. The remaining human legions of Herodius that battled beside them were quickly overcome by the Magi and shepherds.

The demons dispelled, the sacred spires enveloping the battlefield in their holy embrace, Balthazar rose, tentatively but with growing vigor, as the underworldly poisons disintegrated from his veins.

As the acrid mists blew to the desert winds, the hell gate disappeared completely, the remains of the Cage of Domitae rusted and scattered to the wind, the stars calmed above and the earth stopped shaking.

And the Arimathean looked upon the calm of the battlefield, where he had only moments before watched what was left of Herodius being devoured by the same winds, banished into nothingness.

He dropped his swords to the ground.

At long last, vengeance was his.

At long last, peace was his.

FORTY-THREE

"I love you."

Joseph tenderly kissed Mary, and then, gently, kissed the soft, serene face of their newborn.

"And I love you, son."

His arms nestled around her, the baby in her arms. They shed tears of joy, their smiles broken by kisses, to each other, and the boy.

The Magi and shepherds gathered around them, and above them all, the stars and the heavens shone down brightly.

The Arimathean approached them.

He reached into a weathered, sturdy, leather pouch around his waist and removed a small, worn, tenderly mended blanket. He put it to his face, felt it against his lips, clutched it tight against his heart, and handed it to the man and woman.

"The baby may be cold," the Arimathean said. "Swaddle him in this."

Balthazar looked at his friend and put a hand on his shoulder.

The Arimathean averted his gaze, back to the man, woman and child.

Joseph accepted the blanket, placing it over the newborn. He opened his grasp again, inviting the boy's final guardian forward. The Arimathean stepped up and tentatively reached out.

Joseph guided the warrior's grizzled arm to the baby, whose slight, tiny hands clasped and held tight to the mighty paw of the Arimathean.

"You shall forever be blood of his blood," Joseph said to the Arimathean. "Blood of our blood."

The Arimathean nodded, and a wave of contentment washed over him.

They watched over the newborn into the night, until the mother, child and father fell asleep. The Magi, again four, stood sentinel among them, as the shepherds slumbered in the fields, all assembled guarding the three for whom they risked their lives.

In the morning, the Magi bowed before the parents and the child.

"For thirty three days, the heavens will provide us safe haven," Balthazar said. "Our paths shall be masked, our presence unknown.''

"But we must make haste, for while Satan is no more on this mortal plane, and demon spawn cannot enter during this time, Herod will not rest. His soldiers will soon be upon us, meaning to take us captive, for within two years nigh, the heavens will allow him to wreak havoc once more. Therefore, we must escape, travel into exodus, with us as your guides and protectors, into Egypt, into the sacred safe hold of Alexandria, where our agents await."

"And how will we make it there?" Joseph said. "How will we arrive with certainty, safe and unhindered?"

Balthazar approached them.

"I bring frankincense, a potent protector through the spirit planes and our earthly world, and a healing salve when needed."

Melchior and Gaspar both presented items from their cloaks.

"We give you myrrh, which can open and seal the portals between worlds, and allow us to travel unencumbered, to proceed through these earthly realms under invisible means."

And then the Arimathean approached them, slipping off a large leather pouch from his belt.

"And I have gold, in case we need to just bribe our way there."

Joseph and Mary smiled at the four Magi.

"We thank you."

Balthazar looked to the sky, on the horizon.

"We have a considerable journey in front of us, we must go."

The shepherds provided a sturdy cart, which the Magi draped with their cloaks, within which rested Mary and Jesus, the vestments encircled about them, sheltering them and disguising them.

Alongside on each wing traveled Joseph and Melchior, behind the cart trailed Gaspar, and at the fore Balthazar and the Arimathean, on the horses pulling the vehicle.

Their peregrinations spanned the old worlds, across paths foretold, all under the knowing eyes of the glowing bodies in the heavens, which had conspired to bring them together, and now helped protect them.

At long last, they made their way to Egypt, to Alexandria, to safety, and peace.

As they strode towards the city teeming in the distance, the sacred illuminants vigilant above them, lighting the way, the Arimathean turned to Balthazar.

"So what happens now?" the Arimathean said.

"The family will go into hiding within our secret sect here," Balthazar said. "They will be protected, lead as normal a life as possible. They will be sheltered and given all that is needed, and the boy will be raised in the old traditions. In time, he will accompany us to the Glowing City, to continue upon his destined path and expand his training. And then, when the time of exile has passed, they will return to their mother land. Under our protection, of course."

"And that is it?"

"For now," Balthazar said.

"For now," the Arimathean said.

"The world does not change overnight," Balthazar said. "Who would believe it if it did?"

They descended towards Alexandria as the sun reached over the horizon, and at the edge of the town, stopped, to rest, at a dwelling outside of which hung cages bearing a familiar sight.

Doves.

Exotic, beautiful and mysterious.

Black, red and white.

"And so the quest ends, my friend," Balthazar said to the Arimathean. "We are in friendly domains, amidst our own, away from danger."

"So it would seem."

"And you are free to take your own path, away, should you desire."

"Should I desire."

"Or, should you not, you are certainly free to join us, once more."

The Arimathean glared at him, his face stony in false umbrage.

Then, it lightened, and he offered a slight smile.

"And why would I do that?"

"Why would you not?" Balthazar said. "Your vengeance has been gained, your ghosts exorcised, and a whole world awaits, once more, for you to embrace it."

"A world of your faith, I assume," the Arimathean said.

"Or of your own," Balthazar said. "You only need travel upon the path for which you have been destined."

"And what is that?"

"I cannot tell you," Balthazar said, smiling. "Who knows what the future holds? All happens for a reason. But your actions determine those fates you find before you. In the end, the path you take is up to you."

The Arimathean paused, considered, and exhaled deeply.

"You are right," the Arimathean said. "It is."

"Where do you feel your path lies?"

"I do not know," the Arimathean said. "But I have a feeling it may be worth finding out."

Balthazar smiled.

"And that, my friend," he said, "is faith."

The Arimathean grinned and shook his head.

Balthazar laughed.

"My friend, you amaze me, after all you have seen and experienced, to be so stubborn."

"I am not stubborn," the Arimathean grumbled. "Well, yes, maybe a little."

The Arimathean glanced back at the family for whom they, he, had risked all.

"What does it matter anyway, what I think, what I believe?" the Arimathean said. "All that will matter is what the world of men, and those who seek to worship and control and destroy, would choose to believe. In the end, it does not matter at all what I believe."

Balthazar smiled.

"In the end, my friend, it did," Balthazar said. "And in the future, it will."

Gaspar approached them and they looked upon Alexandria sprawled out before them, inviting them in.

"Finally," Gaspar said. "Our journey is over."

The Arimathean looked back at Mary, Joseph, and the infant Jesus, then at the Magi, and ahead at the teeming city of Alexandria.

"It is not over," the Arimathean said. "It has just begun."

EPILOGUE

"So, what do we do now?" Pilate said, fiddling with his rings and downing the last of the wine in his golden goblet, as a servant rushed to fill it again.

"Nothing that can be done," Herod sighed, nervously pacing his palace throne room. "Even Satan said as much. As long as the stars remain in their favor, for the next two years, there is nothing that can be done to harm the child. We could attempt to capture and hold them until that time, but they have fled. To where, we know not. Likely into exile. In two years hence a brief alignment will take place that will allow us to kill him and I will order a purge upon that few days' time, but they will likely know the same and abscond with him away until that window has closed."

Herod drained his wine and an attendant boy was quick to refill the golden chalice in his king's grasp. Herod waited until it was to the brim, then set it down and slapped the slave hard on the face, once, twice, and then slanted his eyes and pursed his lips deviously at the servant and sent him away, the supplicant bowing as he scrambled backwards.

"And then what beyond that two years, if we fail then?" Pilate said.

Herod drank generously, gulped, and breathed out heavily.

"Beyond that, my seers, and Satan himself, have told me that the boy will be safe by the heavens for another thirty years, unable to be killed. So to attempt to do so, until then, will be futile."

Pilate wiped his brow. "And what will you do then? Thirty years hence? They certainly cannot protect him as a child then. He will no doubt begin to testify to his ministry and make himself known, and thereby a much easier target."

Herod chuckled.

"Not to worry, Pilate," he said, climbing the stairs before his throne and seating himself upon it. "We shall be ready, and you shall be prepared."

"In what way? And how should I prepare?"

Herod clapped and looked to his servants, gesturing to them. Fearfully, with great haste, they bowed and jolted from the room. He descended from the throne again, skulking about the space, slowly encircling Pilate.

"You need only prepare by remaining right where you are, my loyal servant, and by doing exactly what I, or, should fate befall me, my heir, advises you to do."

Herod plucked an opulent flower from an arrangement, sniffed it deeply, and crushed it in his fist.

"In the meantime, we will be training and preparing the weapon of our enemy's destruction."

Herod gazed down a long, dark hallway. Pilate's beady eyes followed his. Two servants strode forth from the darkness, and between them, a small boy, no more than five years old, clad in warrior's garb, emerged.

Pilate tittered, breaking into laughs at the sight of the boy.

Herod looked at him and raised an eyebrow with a slight smile.

"A boy? A little boy? And from the looks of him of peasant stock? And he is the engine of destruction for the chosen of the Lord?" Pilate said. He laughed, then raised his goblet to his mouth to partake, pausing it a moment. "I mean you no disrespect, Herod, but surely you joke."

Pilate raised his glass to drink, but stopped, snickering again, letting the goblet linger about his lips.

Herod, smirking, looked at the boy, gave him a subtle nod.

In a lightning shot, the boy yanked a blade from his belt, and whipped it dead on at Pilate's grasp. It impaled the goblet, sending it shooting from his hands, slicing through a vase of flowers, exploding petals bursting into the air in fragrant death, before the knife jagged hard and firm into the wall, still dripping wine and blood as the glass fell, clanging to the floor.

Pilate, breathing heavily and quivering, nursing a slice to his hand, looked petrified at the boy, and then to Herod, who burst out laughing.

"His name is Judas," Herod grinned at Pilate. "Judas Iscariot."

To be continued in

Book Two Of

The Arimathean Trilogy...

The Blood of Destiny

THE ARIMATHEAN TRILOGY

BOOK ONE: THE ARIMATHEAN

BOOK TWO: THE BLOOD OF DESTINY

BOOK THREE: DISINTEGRATION

Question and Answer with Arimathean author Sean Leary

By Connie Corcoran Wilson

Sean Leary has had an eclectic career as a writer, beginning with his first published stories at age 11 in the national newspaper The Comics Buyers Guide. Since then, he has written for scores of newspapers, magazines, websites and blogs. He's written for the theater, television and films, and he's had over two dozen books published.

However, up until now, Leary had never written a novel. His debut in that arena, *The Arimathean*, is as unexpected as it is unique. Whereas Leary's previous works resembled the quirky humor of David Sedaris and Dave Barry or the spiritual and humanistic styles of John Steinbeck and Nick Hornby, *The Arimathean* is an action-adventure tale steeped in speculative historical fiction.

It asks the question 'What if the three Magi and Joseph of Arimathea were ninja wizards sent to protect Jesus, Mary and Joseph from the evil devices of Satan and King Herod?' The book goes on to answer the question, veering from a roller coaster of popcorn movie fun to a thought-provoking meditation on faith.

Leary recently took time out to answer a few questions about *The Arimathean* and his other works.

Q: *The Arimathean* begins with a very unique premise. Where did you get the idea?

A: It actually goes back to my childhood. Having been raised Catholic, my household, during the Christmas season, was always decorated with a Nativity scene. For those unfamiliar with Catholicism, a Nativity scene is a diorama of the birth of Christ. It features a small shack or barn-like structure, and, a manger, where the holy family settled in Bethlehem for the birth of the baby Jesus. It also features a number of modest sized statues, figurines, representing the characters involved in the story.

The figurines are typically plaster or plastic---my family had both, the plaster, which was broken within a few years yielding to a plastic set that lasted much longer – but they featured the same cast of characters: a Joseph, a Mary, a Jesus, a few farm animals, usually a mule and some sheep, and maybe a few camels. Then there would be the handful of shepherds and the angel. And, of course, the three wise men, also known as the three kings or the three Magi.

The figurines, at least in my house, were typically of a size between that of a 'Star Wars' action figure and a Mego Marvel SuperHeroes action figure. As a young boy, I had a decent array of action figures. And, being a young boy, I would come up with various battle scenarios for them. When Christmastime arrived and the Nativity set was unpacked and displayed, I didn't necessarily regard it with the utmost sacrosanct respect that my parents would have liked. Instead, I saw it as an opportunity to add a few new characters to my own mix of imaginary battles.

As such, amidst the 'Star Wars' figures, 'G.I. Joe' guys, Marvel SuperHeroes, Micronauts and other action figures of the time, various Nativity figures would take their place in strange battles I would envision and act out on a daily basis. Luke Skywalker, Spider-Man and Time Traveler would stand beside the three Magi battling against Darth Vader, Baron Karza and the ninja agents of COBRA as they strove to protect or abduct the holy family. I know some thought these war games blasphemous. I found them to be terrific fun. I would venture to guess most pre-teen and elementary school boys – as I was at the time – would agree with me.

As I got older and discovered girls --- and likewise discovered girls weren't impressed by boys who played with action figures, let alone played with Nativity set figurines pretending to be action figures--- I abandoned my war games. But I never forgot them.

Tales of these strange bastardizations of pop culture and Biblical storytelling would come up in conversations with my family over hams and pumpkin pies around the holiday season. Sometimes, this was to embarrass me in front of whatever girl I was dating at the time. But most of the time, it was just good fun. I reminisce today on the goofy and strange things I did when I was a kid.

It was back in the mid-1990s, after a particularly fun and nostalgic Christmas season at home that I got the idea for what would become *The Arimathean*. I was driving home, the two to three hour trek over snowy highways, and my mind began to wander, thinking of the games of my youth, which we had just laughed over minutes earlier, and I began to formulate a story, a really interesting action tale, in which the Nativity scenes I'd envisioned came to life. What if the Magi were warriors sent to protect the holy family? What if they were knights, or soldiers, or, maybe even ninja wizards? I was so excited by it, I ended up pulling over and writing it down, jotting down all the ideas I had. But I didn't really have to worry about forgetting the idea, because I really loved it.

Q: That was back in the mid-1990s. *The Arimathean* as a novel wasn't finished until 2012. What took you so long to complete the novel? Why did you decide to wait?

A: Well, as with most writers and creative people, I have a ton of ideas, and they sort of gestate until one of them demands to be brought to life. *The Arimathean* sort of sat on the backburner, tucked into my brain. From time to time, I would jot ideas for it down into my notebooks. I remember telling my friend and fellow author, Matthew Clemens, about the idea in '98 or so, when we were doing signings for a jam book we collaborated on. He thought it was a great idea. Every time we'd get together he would encourage me to write the darn thing.

Around 2001 I started writing it, chapter by chapter. Over the next eight years it was put together a chapter at a time, in dribs and drabs, always in the background as I was devoting the majority of my time to other projects. In 2009 I started working on it with greater urgency. In the fall of 2011 I began devoting even more time to it. I finished up the first very rough draft in February 2012, a better draft in March 2012, and started polishing it into a final draft during the spring and summer of 2012. From spring to fall 2012, I worked relentlessly on the novel. Every spare moment I got, apart from my substantial time devoted to being a stay-at-home father and an education student getting my masters from the University of Southern California or working to pay the bills was dedicated to *The Arimathean*. I didn't go out on the weekends. I didn't party. I didn't sit around and watch TV when my son was asleep. I worked on my novel. In mid-September 2012 I finally got to the point where I knew it was complete.

Q: You mention Matthew Clemens, who has written a number of books and is a frequent collaborator with Max Allan Collins. The two are best known for their crime fiction works and novelizations of TV shows like "CSI" and "Dark Angel." How did Matthew become involved?

A: Matthew and I have been friends since the mid-'90s and I've always had a terrific amount of respect for him and his talents. He had known about the idea for quite some time. As I said previously, I told him about it back when Clinton was in the White House. He encouraged me to pursue it, feeling it had a lot of potential. Once I started really getting into it, I asked him if he would be so kind as to take a look at the book as I was putting chapters together and as I got a first draft completed. He provided some great advice and a much needed second pair of eyes belonging to someone who is well versed in the craft. His wife, Pam, also read that evolving first draft and provided some terrific advice. As a writer, it's always important to have another reader or two, whether an editor or a friend, because you become so immersed in the work that it's difficult for you to be objective. You lose perspective. Matthew and Pam were excellent beta readers, and I'm very, very grateful to them for all their insight and support along the way. And they're just terrific people. I'm blessed to have them in my life.

Q: What other books or authors influenced you while working on *The Arimathean*?

A: Growing up, there were a number of books that informed my experience as a writer and reader. Having grown up Catholic, one was the Bible. Growing up a geek and fantasy-adventure fan, other significant books, for me, were J.R.R. Tolkien's 'The Lord of the Rings' novels. Others were C.S. Lewis' books and the works of fantasy authors like Michael Moorcock, Edgar Rice Burroughs and Ray Bradbury.

All of them appealed to my nascent imagination with fantastic tales of good versus evil, of amazing creatures and tremendous battles, and of faith winning out against an unrelenting darkness. All of them inform and influence *The Arimethean*, and the stories which will follow in the upcoming books rounding out *The Arimathean trilogy*.

All of the books, from this first volume to the third, are meant to be the type that the younger me would've devoured again and again. I've written them in the hope that other readers will enjoy them the same way.

Q: The characters within the book are Biblically based. You take some liberties with their stories. How much research on the Biblical characters did you do for the book? How much of it is just the product of your imagination?

A: I did do some research, but I didn't base a lot of the book on it. I read the four gospels several times and read the whole of the New Testament twice. So I had a feeling for how to write the book and how to trace the storyline. But it's obvious that I did make a lot of it up. The Magi are only mentioned in one book, the gospel of Matthew, and that's essentially a cameo appearance. Joseph of Arimathea is mentioned in all the gospels, but it's really only in the context of him giving his tomb to Jesus after Christ's death. So there's a lot of leeway taken with those characters. As for the other characters that pop up in the book, again, I had to take a lot of liberties in fleshing them out and making them more complex. I tended to incorporate characters I felt fit the story, as well as those I have always found fascinating, going back to my early years in Catholic school. The Magi, Joseph of Arimathea, John the Revelator, Mary Magdalene, they're all characters I have found to be intriguing in a variety of ways. And then there are characters like the Watchers, the Elohim, who are mentioned in the Old Testament, that I have always found fascinating, so I decided to incorporate them as well.

Q: How did you handle Joseph and Mary? Isn't it a slippery slope you're walking, writing them as real people, as human beings with feelings and concerns that are realistic given the situations, while trying not to offend any believers?.

A: I was raised Catholic, and I still consider myself a Christian and a faithful believer in God. I wrote the characters with a lot of respect for them and consideration for how they were portrayed. I based a lot of their characteristics on the writings in the Bible. I tried to write from their perspectives in regard to what they went through, and the things I made up, the dialogue I made up, was all with due respect and portrays them as good, moral people. A lot of their characteristics to paint them as complex characters are based upon the gospels. I figured that every child, even Jesus, is influenced by his parents and by the way they're raised. So I took certain details from Jesus' sermons and parables and extrapolated them and applied them to form the backstories of Mary and Joseph. That way, it honors the Biblical material and also makes sense from a familial perspective. I'm not out to offend anyone. I'm trying to tell a story that is entertaining to read from a fantasy and adventure perspective and has a moral core to it that resonates as an echo of its source material and resonates with believers today as well. This is really no different than someone making a film like "Jesus of Nazareth" or "The Passion of the Christ" or "Jesus Christ

Superstar." The source material is reflected, but you also have to take liberties along the way in making up dialogue or adding scenes or actions to tell a fuller story.

Q: How is your own religious background reflected?

A: I went to Catholic elementary and junior high schools, a Catholic high school and a Catholic university through my first year of college before I transferred to a state university. I lapsed from the Catholic Church, but never abandoned my belief in Christ and certainly not my faith in God. That's where I remain today. I attend a variety of Christian churches because I believe they each have different things to offer. I can't say I adhere to a specific branch of religious faith, but I believe in the basic tenets involved, the golden rule of loving God and loving one another that Christ espoused. And, even through all the ninjas and such in the book, you see that faith reflected.

Q: How is faith reflected?

A: The Arimathean, the character, is really an allegory for humanity and man's struggle with faith. The characters within the book represent different belief structures. Their dialogue reflects that. The Arimathean himself asks a lot of tough questions that I think almost everyone has asked in regard to God's place on earth and in their lives and in the role of humanity. Balthazar represents faith. His answers realistically reflect the answers I often got in Catholic school when I would ask the priests and teachers similar questions.

Q: How much research did you do regarding the time period? Is the book a realistic portrayal of the era?

A: Not much historical research beyond the re-examination of the Bible. It's not what I would call a painstakingly realistic representation of the historical period. I began to research it, but the more I did, the more I came across things that didn't serve the story well, so I decided to eliminate the minute details and instead paint with broad strokes to capture a feel for the time. It feels like a Biblical epic. It has the details we've come to expect from Biblical stories, whether in films or on TV. I was more concerned with just telling a really compelling story on a number of levels and less concerned with things like whether or not they would've realistically been riding horses or camels or walking on foot. Horses just fit the story best, so they're on horses. If the characters are traveling a long distance and being attacked by demons and Roman centurions, it made more sense to me to have them on horses rather than on foot. If you want to read a breathtakingly researched, photo-realistic look at the time period, look elsewhere. If you want to read a fun action story with ninjas and demons and magic and monsters that also has some intriguing and thought-provoking dialogue, this is the book for you.

Q: The book has some particularly violent and gory sequences. Other sequences are quite beautiful and uplifting. What led you to emphasize the violence?

A: To create tension. To create a sense of fear, a sense of danger. Think about it: Almost every reader is going to come into this book knowing the end of the story. The challenge for me was to create suspense and tension in a story where you already know the ending. So I have to really ramp up the evil they face, really ramp up the obstacles and the opposition. I needed to get readers to the point where I create enough tension and suspense that they might actually ask themselves, 'If he's changing things up this much, is he going to change the ending? Is he actually going to kill off one of these characters or do something really crazy at the end?' At the very least, I just wanted readers to have fun reading the story, and to create that roller coaster you need to have really powerful and strong heroes and maybe even stronger villains and great opposition for those heroes to overcome. That's what creates the tension and gets people hooked. That's what keeps people reading.

Q: The book is very cinematic. Do you see it as a movie?

A: The way I typically write stories, whether as part of a novel or short stories, is I envision them in my head as movies. I try to describe what I'm seeing in my head for the reader. So, yeah, of course I see *The Arimathean* as a film. And, yeah, of course, like a lot of authors, I would love to see my book as a movie. I know some books don't work as films, but action and fantasy translates particularly well to the big screen, especially when you're dealing with otherworldly powers and creatures and a broader canvas. I think *The Arimathean trilogy* would make a terrific set of films. Or, at least, they make a great set of films in my imagination, as I'm seeing them in my head.

Q: If, as you say, you see the story as a film in your head as you're writing it, what actors would you cast?

A: Really there were only two that I recognized, to be honest. For example, the Joseph and Mary in my head, the Balthazar in my head, were people that I have never seen before. So they're actors in the theater company of my own imagination. One I would cast is Dwayne Johnson, the Rock, as Gaspar. He just has the right presence and look to be Gaspar, and he's got the action star background. I think he'd be great casting in that part. The other is Hugh Jackman as The Arimathean. I think Hugh Jackman is a phenomenal actor. He would be perfect for the title role in all three movies. But, you know, that's sort of a pipe dream at this point, wishful thinking!

Q: What do you see the future holding for *The Arimathean*? You mention it's the first in a trilogy, how is the trilogy going to play out?

A: When I first got the idea, it was for a massive novel that began with the birth of Christ and ended far in the future with the second coming and the apocalypse. It's basically following the story of the New Testament – it begins with the birth of Christ in the gospels and ends with the end of the world in Revelation. As I began writing chapters and refining my thinking about it, it made the most sense to break it up into a trilogy. So that's what I've done. The first book, *The Arimathean*, takes place in the days just prior to and after the birth of Christ. The second book, which I'm writing right now, tentatively called *The Blood of Destiny,* takes place around the time of the death of Christ. And the third book, tentatively titled *DisIntegration*, takes place in the future, around 2033 and involves the apocalypse and the second coming.

So in essence, the first two books cover the gospels and the last book is Revelation. However, I take great liberties with all of them and tell very different stories while retaining the same general outlines. As for when the trilogy will be complete, I don't know. I'm writing the very rough draft of the second book right now. I have an outline and a few chapters of the third book. But they're far from being done. I don't have any set date to finish or any release dates for the second and third books in the trilogy. I'm going to write the best books I possibly can, tell the most entertaining and imaginative stories I can, and when I feel I've done my best, they'll be released. I can say that I'm extremely excited about being immersed in writing the trilogy and that, unlike the first book, the second and third won't take more than a decade to become reality. When all are done and released, I hope they form a terrific trilogy that pleases readers and keeps them coming back, again and again. And, at every turn, I hope they enjoy them. Really, that's what it's all about. I want people to enjoy reading the books. I want kids like me, book fans like I was as a kid, to love *The Arimathean trilogy* the same way I loved those C.S. Lewis and Tolkien and Burroughs books I read as a kid.

Q: Any last thoughts?

A: I just want to say thank you to anyone who bought the book, anyone who read it, and I hope they enjoyed it. In however small a way I hope it made their life better for having read it, even if just as entertainment. And if you did enjoy it, please tell your friends to check it out! I hope people enjoy the books, and I thank you for reading them.

Connie Corcoran Wilson (www.ConnieCWilson.com) is an award-winning writer, a Featured Contributor to Yahoo!, the David R. Collins Midwest Writing Center Writer of the Year (March 20, 2010) and was the Associated Content Writer of the Year in 2009. She has written more than two dozen books, her latest being "The Color of Evil," (www.TheColorOfEvil.com).

Other Books By Sean Leary

Does The Shed Skin Know It Was Once A Snake? (short stories)

Every Number Is Lucky To Someone (short stories)

Exorcising Ghosts (graphic novel)

Beautiful Remnants of Chaotic Failures (poetry)

Here Comes The Goot! (children's/beginning readers)

My Life As A Freak Magnet (humor/memoir)

FOR MORE WRITING AND MORE INFORMATION,
SEE WWW.SEANLEARY.COM AND
WWW.THEARIMATHEAN.COM.

THANK YOU FOR READING
THE ARIMATHEAN...

13938940R00212

Made in the USA
San Bernardino, CA
11 August 2014